Hobson's Choice
& 15 other twist-in-the-tail short stories

Clive West

ALSO BY THIS AUTHOR

The Road

Lymphedema – Living with the disease

Find a job and get it

Published by Any Subject Books (www.anysubject.com)

Copyright © 2012 Clive West & Any Subject Books

ISBN: 978-1-909392-00-7

Disclaimer: This is a work of fiction. Any resemblance of characters to actual persons, living or dead, is purely coincidental.

CONTENTS

FOREWORD

It's one of those wearisome and pretentious forewords, you're thinking. Well, perhaps it is and, in which case, you are hereby given permission to skip the page and move straight on to the stories. However, if you'd like to know a bit more about what drove me to write them, then do read on as I hope that you'll then get more from your reading. You also have my promise that I'll try to walk a tightrope between giving away spoilers and being too elliptical.

A good education is a period piece and it draws on my own direct personal experience of bullying in an English public school. With its dark and sinister passageways, constant bullying, and sadistic teachers, such a place would not be somewhere I'd ever send a child (although I recognise that times have now changed).

Hobson's choice centres around my lifelong interest in how seemingly small and insignificant events can become major forks in our passage through life. It's a chilling and dark story which I personally consider to be among the strongest that I've ever written. I hope my readers find it thought-provoking.

I wrote *Dear John* as a cautionary account aimed at those who are busy making plans that rely upon the good intentions of others. No-one, no matter how close they are to you, will ever have exactly the same agenda as you. So, be warned.

It is said the present is the key to the past and the future and I've come to subscribe to this point of view. I firmly believe that our emotions, desires and propensity to commit acts of both good and evil, are largely unchanged in tens of thousands of years, and if our species survives that long, will be the same as they are now thousands of years hence. The technology may change but the end user and all their imperfections will not.

My two Sci-Fi stories - *Lucky charm* and *The return of the Centaurus* - both reflect this reasoning and I have steered away from describing fantastical gadgetry in favour of a study of how humans might cope in the situations that the technology gives rise to.

Although a staunch scientist and confirmed non-believer in such things, I do love a good ghost story, and I remember the eager anticipation I had for the BBC's 'Ghost story for Christmas'. This was always a production based on one of the eerie tales written by the talented M R James. *An enduring smile, The racing line, Seeing is believing* as well as *A good education* all have a supernatural air about them.

Spaghetti westerns were the success story of my childhood and Sergio Leone created some vile 'bad guys' who you knew would meet suitably unpleasant ends. The bad guy being the one with a black hat (in a metaphorical sense if not a literal one) has since been done to death and something more subtle is required for the modern reader. I've derived great pleasure from dreaming up some bad guys of my own and then finding alternative endings to the 'grand finale shoot out'. Both *Every one a winner* and *Moving up* deal with greed and what it can make people do, while

Last orders, Seeing is believing and *A day at the beach* look at other dark facets of the human psyche.

The logical consequences of the lynch mobs which gather outside some high profile criminal trials has always troubled me. The "Hang 'em high" brigade usually want to string up the defendant long before the trial has got past the preamble stage but the whole idea of a trial is to establish guilt – something which explains the 'not guilty' option for juries. Punishing the wrong person (as has occasionally been known to happen) is not just wrong in itself, it also sends a dangerous message to the real perpetrator. This is why the making of snap and ill-informed judgements bothers me.

To show what I mean, *The watcher* and the much more gentle, *Lost* are warnings to those who would be hasty in forming such opinions. *No walk in the park* is another chip off this block although coming at the idea from a very different angle.

On a different note, The bench could be a stage play with the whole story being centred around an ordinary park bench. It's an idea I've been throwing around in my head for sometime now and it harks back to the way in which I perceive fate as being a tangled web of probability lines.

So, those are my tales and I hope that you derive as much pleasure from reading them as I have done from writing them.

Clive West

Italy, January 2012

A GOOD EDUCATION

The grey and austere walls of the Mercer's School for Boys seemed better suited to crushing the spirit rather than building it. Well, that was the humble opinion of one of the humblest members of its fraternity. Mornington, like the London underground station, nicknamed 'Moon' as a consequence of his mind's tendency to disappear into outer space during lessons, had just turned thirteen, that early Autumn of 1961.

The bell chimed for the end of the mid-morning break, however Moon was never quite sure whether the sound was to be welcomed or dreaded. The pealing signified the end of the period of organised bullying by his peers, but the commencement of the period of more subtle but equally sadistic bullying by his teachers. It seemed as if there was never any reprieve.

Along with his classmates, he scurried down the dark, oppressive corridors with their broken tiled floors that must have carried countless thousands of other wretched individuals during the school's five centuries of existence. His father had attended Mercer's (and hence his own enrolment) but his father had been a member of the first fifteen 'rugger' team, a corporal in the military training that the school proudly practised, and had excelled at just about everything.

In fact his father's old military uniform still fitted the old man's ramrod-straight back superbly, and no matter how physical an activity he engaged in while wearing it, no crease ever dared to appear.

Moon had attempted to appeal to his father about what life was like at Mercer's. He'd tried to describe the daily beatings he got from other pupils and the frequent thefts of exercise books from his locker that would leave him in hot water with his teachers over his missing homework. His father had merely given him a speech about how it was 'the same in his day,' had 'never done anyone any harm' and was all a 'bit of high spirits and horseplay'.

Even when a boy had drowned in the river the previous year, no-one seemed to want to question it. The incident was 'clearly' just a tragic accident and that was an end to it. Talk of the local Chief Constable being an Old Boy like Moon's father had been rife in the school but no-one had been certain of the rumour's veracity.

Moon suspected differently. He had not known the boy, Bodkins, particularly well, but he did know with the absolute confidence of a kindred spirit that Bodkins had been bullied just like he was being. That said, there was no point voicing this opinion as it would only get him into more trouble with his housemaster and, perhaps, even with the headmaster.

Moon was already on permanent detention which meant he had to place a pink report card in front of the teacher before every lesson. In a particularly despicable effort to gain cheap popularity, some of his teachers would then ask his classmates what grade they thought Moon merited for his participation and performance – something which inevitably resulted in him getting a 'D' or an 'E' on his card. Naturally, these low grades would get him into even more trouble.

What lay behind Moon's apparent lack of concentration was that he heard voices. It wasn't anything spectral – no, he didn't believe in ghosts or such, those were just silly stories set to frighten. His voices made suggestions about ideas and inventions that usually had no connection to the lesson going on around him. There was the rub.

For example, he was in a Latin lesson and the unfortunate phenomenon had begun. He was sat in the middle row, a place he secretly hoped would keep him apart from the back-row bullies and securely out of the mind of Mr Smallett, his teacher.

"Puer non puella amaverit," droned Smallett. "What is wrong with that statement?" He paused briefly while his bird-of-prey's eyes scanned the room looking for his next victim. "Mornington?"

Realising that they were all off the hook, the rest of the class turned in relief towards Moon who was busy sketching a plan of a house that used the sun to provide heat for …

"Mornington! Are you awake, boy?" Smallett ranted, a globule of spittle hitting a boy in the front row who didn't dare be seen to wipe it from his face.

"Yes, sir," Moon answered with a shiver. Questions weren't good and were to be avoided at all costs.

"Well, if you're sure that we're not taking up too much of your valuable time," Smallett said sarcastically, using his hands, comedian-like, to invite peals of laughter from the other boys. "Perhaps you would care to enlighten us with the answer."

Moon's stomach dropped to the floor, what was the stupid question? He hadn't even known there was one. "Um, could you repeat the question, please, sir?" he asked.

"Yes, of course, Mornington, I'd be delighted to run it by you again – see you afterwards for detention. Does any boy know the answer or, heaven forbid, do I have a class full of Morningtons?"

There was more raucous laughter and, while Smallett was writing the answer on the board, a few boys threw inky paper at Moon. Yet another detention, he groaned. It was rapidly getting to the crazy stage where he just couldn't fit them all in. He'd probably end up with a detention because he couldn't do all the detentions. Mercer's ran on that kind of logic.

The rest of the day went much to programme. As per normal, he was pushed back and back in the lunch queue and this made him so late getting to the food counter that the middle-aged, sour-faced kitchen lady had completely run out of the main course. She shrugged her shoulders, gave her best 'what's this got to do with me?' look, and dumped a portion of stodgy jam roll and tepid lumpy custard into his chipped white china bowl. He then had to bolt the food down to avoid being late for his lunchtime detention.

Lunchtime detentions usually consisted of picking up paper, sweeping the quadrangle, or carrying books or boxes for one of the masters. It all depended upon who was on duty. Some teachers were reasonably lenient but there were others like his housemaster who clearly found great amusement in thinking up new and ever more vicious punishments.

Today was the day that his housemaster was on duty, the thought of which made Moon groan again. This was going to be bad, he just knew it. Still, there was no point in him trying to think of an evasion tactic. All that would happen would be the addition of interest, making the punishment even more brutal.

"Get into your PE kit, boy. You have precisely three minutes or you'll be doing it this evening as well," boomed his Draculian housemaster, Mr Catford.

"Yes, sir," Moon shuddered, he hated sports. Without waiting for further comment, he sped off in the direction of the changing rooms. At least there wouldn't be any other boys there to throw him in the showers or tip Wellington boots of term-old urine over his clothes.

"You're late, boy," Catford groused on Moon's return a fraction over 180 seconds later. "This is my break you're taking up, do you realise that, boy?"

"Yes, sir. I'm sorry, sir," Mornington stuttered.

"You are to do the junior's cross-country run," Catford said with obvious relish. "And, just in case you're thinking of taking any short cuts, be warned that I'll be checking up on you even though you won't be able to see me." He bent down to stare direct into Moon's eyes. "Do you hear me, boy?"

"Yes, sir."

"I had the pleasure to teach your father and I'm disappointed to say what a disgrace you are to your family name," he paused as if searching for an even more damning epithet. "Off you go, I can't stand looking at you any longer."

Moon started off at a steady trot. His asthma meant that to go any faster would be to court a nasty attack of coughing. Mind, he had made the mistake of using that once as an excuse for coming in late and then had been given another detention for his trouble.

The short cross-country route took him around the playing fields, through some light woodland, and then down to the river which he followed to the school driveway bridge. The remainder of the route was back along the driveway to the original starting point.

As usual, when he was alone, he started hearing the voices in his head. There were ideas for paintings, cars that could go at incredible velocities on virtually no fuel, and houses that were always warm despite the weather outside.

No-one had ever seen these ideas since there was nowhere safe to write them down. He had once tried recording them in a journal but it had been discovered by some boys who had promptly forced him to tear it up into very small pieces. When he had used an art lesson to paint an idea, another boy had tipped a jam-jar of murky water over the picture he had painstakingly reproduced from the one in his head. The teacher, who had witnessed the episode, had been angry with him for making a mess and wasting school materials and, to complete the unhappy experience, had written an 'E' on Moon's report card.

The wood was dangerous territory. Too often first and second year boys had been kidnapped and taken there by fifth formers and the casually-clad upper and lower sixth. There were lots of stories of boys being tied to trees and then used for darts practice, or even worse. Mornington wasn't sure what the 'worse' was but the few boys he knew who had suffered such an ordeal all seemed so traumatised afterwards that not one of them was prepared to talk about their experiences no matter how much they were cajoled.

As he turned along the river, he suddenly felt a stronger than normal presence in his head. This wasn't the usual friendly and gentle professor who gave him his ideas, this was an icy blast that seemed to occupy his whole body. It was so strong that he shuddered with the cold even though his exertions and the September sunshine were striving to make him hot and sweaty.

Moon couldn't explain what happened next. An image came into his head, every bit as clear as one of the Disney movies that the boys were occasionally allowed to watch as a treat. Unlike his normal 'messages' which were disembodied, characterless voices, this one was loud, clear and very angry. Not only that, this time he could see as well as hear the voice. Well, it wasn't so much that he could see the person speaking; it was more like a running radio commentary accompanying some silent film footage.

In his head, he saw a group of older boys throwing mud at a smaller and younger boy who was standing on the towpath and trying to protect his face from the onslaught. Behind the boys and egging them on was Catford who even picked up and threw a few sticks himself. As the group closed in on him, the boy fell into the fast-flowing river (there seemed a lot more water in it than today) and disappeared from sight.

Moon could even hear the boy screaming as he fought a losing battle to get breath, and he felt a crushing pain in his chest which he first mistakenly thought was an imminent asthma attack. He could also hear Catford instructing the group to say the boy had fallen in while they were some way away and that they had tried heroically in vain to save him but it had been too late.

Suddenly the vision disappeared and he was back to jogging along the towpath with the river flowing sleepily past him in the September sunshine. The voice in his head hadn't gone although its tone had changed with the end of the film footage. It now chatted away about all the things it would like to do, places it would like to see, and its aspirations for the future. His uninvited companion stayed with him the entire length of the riverbank right up until Moon came to the bridge. At this point the voice told him it would be going in a different direction from Moon and it bade him a friendly, but somehow forlorn, farewell.

Feeling slightly puzzled and drained by the experience, Moon returned to school just in time to get a quick shower and head off for his afternoon's lessons. There had happily been no sign of Catford – no doubt he was far too busy lording it up in the teachers' lounge.

Since Catford was the duty detention master for the whole week and sending Moon off on a pointless cross-country run was a soft option for him, the punishment became a regular daily event. Still, at least the run meant that he was free from attacks by other boys. He consoled himself with that thought as he stumbled along the track.

It was on his third such run of the week that the voice returned but this time it came without the snippet of film footage. It felt to Moon as if the boy who'd fallen in the river was now talking to him from somewhere in the darker recesses of his own head.

The voice was friendly but forceful. It was telling him over and over again that the only way to put an end to the bullying was for him to go on the offensive. It stressed that passively taking the punishment each day was not the answer. The voice was weirdly convincing, as if it spoke with great authority on the matter, however it was the diametric opposite to the occasional advice he had had from his father about acquiring a 'stiff upper lip' and 'taking it like a man'.

The voice didn't stop with just the message; it continued to lay out detailed plans for exactly what he should do. Once it had all been explained to him, it seemed so delightfully obvious. How come he'd never considered a similar idea before?

Saturday's detention, while everyone else had 'rec', was to help Mr Workton, the middle-aged and prematurely balding English teacher who always smelt of stale cigarette smoke and alcohol. The two of them had to produce the programmes for the forthcoming Lower School Parents and Teachers evening. These pamphlets consisted of the dates and titles of next term's plays (plus how you could buy tickets), details of optional (but highly recommended) out-of-school activities (more purchases) and lists of various 'must-have' items that were exclusively for sale in the school sports shop. In essence, it was a thinly disguised and rather tacky attempt at squeezing more money out of parents.

The programmes were to be printed on the geriatric school Gestetner, a satanic-looking device which permanently resided in the corner of the school secretary's office. She was not in on Saturday so therefore she would be unable to object to the chaotic mess that her normally spick and span refuge would be transformed into.

Although Moon was really only supposed to be passing paper to Mr Workton (the Gestetner had been declared much too dangerous for children to operate) and stacking up the printed sheets after the ink had dried, his English teacher soon had him working the machine on his own.

"There you go, lad. Just keep printing 'em until you've done 150 copies and then change the sheet on the roller and do 150 of that one and so on. When you've finished, staple them together and put 'em all neatly into those boxes," he patted Moon on the back so hard that he nearly knocked the pint-sized boy into the machine.

"I'm just nipping out for some, um, fresh air," he explained awkwardly, "I'll be back soon if anyone needs me."

I know that you're going down The Bell and that you won't come back until they've thrown you out or you're plastered or, more likely both, thought Moon. He had heard that word from one of the Sixth Formers who knew just about everything there was to know about life, and he liked it. Plastered, plastered, plastered, he said to himself.

It was as he was contemplating the thought that his running companion jolted him back to reality. "Don't forget!" it sternly reminded Moon, and then disappeared again.

Moon conscientiously worked his way through the hundreds of sheets. It took him several hours but there was still no sign of Mr Workton nor, if he was to run to habit, was there likely to be for an hour or so yet. The jet-black ink was getting everywhere and Moon knew he would be in trouble for the damage to his school uniform. Now wasn't the time to worry over that, he decided, dismissing the fear from his mind.

He sat down at the secretary's desk, and opened her drawers one-by-one, ignoring the half-eaten pack of chocolate raisins, and skipping past the files on a few boys who had recently been expelled. Finally he found what he was looking for - the blank Gestetner sheets. Picking up a biro, he proceeded to carefully fill the page with the story his friend had narrated to him. After he had done that, he placed the sheet on the Gestetner and then ran off 150 copies.

When he'd finished all the printing, he stapled the sheets together, making sure to include his extra page towards the end of each programme. He saved one copy which he folded over twice before placing it in an envelope addressed using information he'd got from a file he found in the cabinet marked 'former students'.

He took a postage stamp from the sheet in the secretary's drawer and stuck it on the envelope which he then dropped in the outgoing post-tray. The letter would be sent by first class post on Monday.

The Parents and Teachers' Meeting was scheduled for Friday evening and Moon's detentions that week consisted of moving chairs, erecting directional signs, and generally making sure that no surface bore any trace of its usual grime. It was hard and thankless work. No matter how fast he moved, one or the other of the duty masters would invariably berate him for his slackness.

The day arrived and the parents filed into Mercer's Congregational Hall where they were to sit for a few minutes (more like an hour) while the headmaster gave a short speech (droned on) about the progress of Old Boys, the troubling state of the chapel roof, and the benefits of (paid for) extra-curricular activities for widening the horizons of young and growing minds.

After that, parents would be encouraged to wander around the school, meeting the various Form Teachers and viewing selected boys' work, while the headmaster would be on hand to discuss and receive promises of donations and endowments.

The audience was no sooner seated than a muttering started among some of the parents. Unaccustomed to this kind of indiscipline in the ranks, the headmaster grew increasingly concerned until this emotion turned into complete panic as some parents, enraged at what they had just read, stood up waving their programmes at him 'demanding to know the meaning of it'. The headmaster was completely baffled as to what the 'it' in question was. He only found out after one angry parent had thrust a programme in his face and he had surreptitiously nipped behind the stage curtain to seek refuge and to read it.

Under 'Essay of the Term' was a story entitled 'A personal account of my drowning by S. Bodkins'. The story made abundantly clear that this drowning was neither a tragic accident nor the sad suicide of a boy lacking in sufficient moral fibre to withstand the well-intentioned banter and buffoonery that went with such an elite education as Mercer's provided.

The headmaster was just in the process of denying everything when two more parents walked in. They had not been formally invited but they had received a copy of the same handwritten essay through the mail.

"As I was saying,... as I was saying everybody, this is just some over-active child's mind combined with an inappropriate sense of humour. I can assure you that there is no truth in it whatsoever. Now, if I may have your attention, please, ladies and gentlemen, I would like to return ..."

The headmaster's voice trailed off to pained silence as a pair of white-faced parents pushed their way to the front and on to the dais. They were Mr and Mrs Bodkins.

"Yes, headmaster, do continue denying how our son, Stevie, was bullied mercilessly while your housemaster looked on and even participated. Do explain why you needed to pull strings to cover this up. Do explain what you told the police to stop them from treating this 'tragic accident' as a cold-blooded murder. We'd love to hear," Mr Bodkins spoke quietly but, by that time, a pin could have been heard on its way to the ground. His words were without tone or expression yet they managed to convey deep   emotion.

"I'm sorry, Mr Bodkins but your son's death was a tragic accident and I see nothing in this prank essay to change that view," the headmaster snapped. He knew he was losing it, and even if he had to make the Bodkins family out as villains of the piece, something must be done to save face in front of this amassed rank of parents.

"You murdered our son," sobbed Mrs Bodkins pointing at the housemaster.

"Now really, Mrs Bodkins. That is an extremely serious accusation and you should consider the implications of slandering the good name of our housemaster in front of so many people." The headmaster was sweating heavily. Damn, why were there so many lights on this stupid stage?

"A murder is not 'a prank' nor is it slander to tell the truth. This essay is a statement written as if by our dead son and somehow in his handwriting. I don't care how it's happened but it has and I want justice for our boy."

At that point Moon thought Mr Bodkins was about to murder either the headmaster or the housemaster or even maybe both of them. He certainly looked in the mood to do it. However, before that could happen pandemonium broke out. Several women fainted and there were angry shouts from the fathers. Mr Bodkins stood there transfixing the, now silent, headmaster with his eyes.

Later that week there was an extraordinary meeting of the Board of Governors who voted unanimously to remove the headmaster, implement a fierce anti-bullying campaign, and fully co-operate with the police in their re-opened manslaughter investigation. The housemaster and the boys who had been present at the drowning were instantly suspended pending the outcome of the enquiry and, wherever they ended up, they certainly never returned to Mercer's school.

Under the new and much more liberal regime, Mornington's designs were regularly commended by the replacement art and design teacher but, for some strange reason, he never heard any more voices.

THE WATCHER

The girls in the Minton Upper School playground were thankfully oblivious to his presence – that was a key part of Gerry's design. It would only serve to spoil everything if they knew about him. He wanted them 'au naturel' and not playing to the gallery.

For what must have been the tenth time he wiped the perspiration off his binoculars and hoped to goodness that they hadn't alerted the girls by glinting in the fierce early summer sunshine.

Getting a room with a decent view had not been easy. Fortunately, Gerry had eventually found a gentleman who nodded understandingly when he said he wanted to observe the girls 'in camera'. The man even went so far as to suggest that they shared a common interest. Perhaps they should get together for a chat later, Gerry mused, allowing himself a wry smile as he did so. For the moment, though, he had a strictly one-track mind.

It would have been good to get nearer. Watching the girls coming out from their lessons at lunchtime and seeing them milling around the playground from the far side of a busy road was not ideal, but he would have attracted unwanted attention if he'd sat in his car. Besides which, it was all double yellows anyway, and he didn't need a traffic warden nosily querying his activities. Still, it didn't stop him wishing he were there in the school and among the action.

Seeing some of the girls perched on the walls eating their lunch made him hungry and he reached for one of the ham salad sandwiches his wife had carefully packed for him this morning. She had no idea when she made them that he would be eating them squeezed between boxes of pack-rat junk in a dirty bedroom watching girls the age of their daughter. What would she say?

It was just something he had to do.

But, then, this was not the first occasion that Gerry had observed these particular girls, although it was the first time he had sat outside their school. And, while his eyes were everywhere, his attention was really focussed on two or three girls in particular. This small group had interested him in a way the others didn't and he followed them with his binoculars, careful not to miss any detail of their activities.

Suddenly he was distracted by a couple of boys – well, young men, really - who were probably only two or three years older than the most senior girls in the playground. One of them whistled loudly (Gerry could hear the shrill sound above the traffic) and three girls ambled over. It looked just like a scene from Grease – one of his daughter's favourite films.

There was clearly a lot of sexual tension, with the girls especially savouring their roles as young temptresses. Gerry watched, fixated by the scene that was being played out in front of him. Two of the girls flashed glimpses of their underwear at the boys who, in turn, made jumping motions, holding their crotches as they leapt. One girl, bolder than the others, leant over the bars and gave her boyfriend (Gerry supposed) a long, lingering kiss. No prizes for guessing what they would be doing this evening, he thought – it hadn't been like that in his day.

The boys eventually left to a chorus of whistles, catcalls and more flashed underwear.

At that moment the door of the room he was in suddenly opened. Gerry span around, irritated by the unwanted interruption, to see his host holding two mugs of tea and a packet of Rich Tea biscuits. He was also carrying a magazine between his fingers. It was intriguingly titled, 'Young and Fresh'. It looked to Gerry like it had been well-thumbed.

"Thought I might join you – know what I mean," the man said, tapping his nose with his finger.

"I prefer to be alone if it's all the same," Gerry snapped, snubbing the offer of company.

The man laughed bawdily, "You don't need to be shy with me. I reckon we understand one another good enough. After all, a man can't help getting a boner watching those little tarts." He paused, seemingly for dramatic effect. "Most of them are begging for it, you know," he continued, tapping his nose again as he said the words.

"I prefer to just watch …. alone", Gerry looked away from the man, shunning him and effectively blocking off any further discussion.

"Well, I was just being sociable, there's no need to snap," the man said peevishly. "I'll leave the tea and biscuits here, then. You can help yourself." He put the mug and packet down on one of the many cardboard boxes, the tea slopping over the side of the chipped china. Without waiting to mop up the spillage, he shuffled off back the way he had come, grumbling to himself about ungrateful people.

The man's unwelcome appearance had proved a distraction in more ways than one. Now, for some sudden and inexplicable reason, Gerry felt the need to relieve himself and he wished he had the wherewithal to do so without leaving his garret. It would have to wait – having come this far, he wasn't prepared to risk missing anything. There might not be another such good opportunity as this.

It would, of course, be better if he could get the girls he was fascinated by on their own but that was just not going to be viable – not yet, anyway. He had that planned for later. That's when it would really get interesting. This was just the preliminary part – the first phase, so to speak.

The girls he was after making the acquaintance of were particularly confident, striding purposefully around as the other girls deferentially made way for them. There was even a small entourage of younger girls who followed them everywhere; they were of little interest but, nevertheless, they would still need to be isolated later. It complicated the plan slightly but even the best plans were made to be adapted, he told himself.

Gerry took another bite of his sandwich, choosing to ignore his host's hospitality. Cramp had set in to his knees and legs and he groaned silently to himself. Next time he should really bring something comfortable to kneel on, or take a fisherman's stool with him, for example.

The end of playtime was approaching and in fifteen minutes the girls would be back in their classrooms. After that happened, there would sadly be nothing further to see and he would just have to make arrangements for another day. If that did happen, he could honestly say that today hadn't been a complete waste of time but he would still be far from satisfied with the return on his efforts.

Just as Gerry was contemplating the possibility of a fruitless day, a black coupe with darkened windows pulled up and a man, the passenger, got out. He peered around, seemed satisfied, and ran to the fence where one of the girls snatched a small package from him, swiftly lifted up her skirt and then, quite unselfconsciously, tucked the parcel into her underwear.

The passenger didn't wait to feast his eyes on the display of young thighs. He was back in the car long before she had given Gerry a full-frontal display of what his wife would have called 'next week's washing'.

Acting by instinct and from years of training, Gerry dropped the binoculars, snatched up the microphone that he had hidden in his pack and shouted into it, "Now!, Now! Now!"

A split-second later, two cars screeched around the corner from behind the school and swung diagonally across the road in front of the coupe. Meantime, two substitute teachers suddenly brandished warrant cards and raced to intercept the girl who had received the package. Also on hand was a bespectacled lady from Child Services who was there to protect the interests of the girl although, if pressed on the matter, Gerry would have struggled to consider the young lady an innocent.

It had all gone to plan. All that was left now were the

interviews to conduct and then the obligatory reports to write up. It wasn't entirely glamour, Gerry reminded himself.

However, before he could leave the dive that he'd spent the day in, there was just a small matter of having a man-to-man chat with the landlord about his particular taste in reading material.

Gerry shivered at the prospect. He couldn't wait to get home.

MOVING UP

Jason switched off the radio and turned it over to play one of the CD's that he had purposefully bought that morning. Personally he couldn't stand what was collectively called 'modern music' – house, garage, trance, rap etc. It was all 'jungle noise' to him. In any case, he'd only bought the damned things to annoy the neighbours with. As soon as he had succeeded in his aim, and that was well underway now, they were all going straight in the nearest bin. Here goes, he thought – full volume, windows down, sun-roof open – the last mile of his journey home.

Home. Home was a very ordinary, 1940's terraced box stuck roughly in the middle of a small row of other ugly 1940's terraced boxes on the inside edge of a very bad bend that had become an accident black spot. The houses had little to commend them, he considered. Well, little except for their large gardens and the field behind.

It had been a real step down, moving into one of these terminally unappealing boxes, but it was a necessary evil. His real house was in the country – en-suite bathrooms, indoor swimming pool, mezzanines, and surrounded by lawns and courtyards. At the moment it was both rented out and mortgaged to the hilt in order to finance his latest scheme.

Driving past the row of terraced houses one day, Jason had noticed that the middle one was up for sale. With growing interest, he had pulled over and eyed up this sorry little group of dwellings. They had two things in their favour – they were all set well back from the road and they all had huge rear gardens. During the war years, when the houses had been hastily erected to accommodate bombed-out townies, these gardens had presumably been intended as 'Dig for Victory' allotments but now they were just overgrown, weed-choked eyesores.

At the time he drove past, Jason had been looking around for his next investment and this had seemed perfect. He privately fancied himself as a bit of a property developer and he had already made money renovating and selling a couple of old houses that he had chanced upon. The profit obtained from flipping these had allowed him to put in the necessary down-payment on his house in the country with a small amount of working capital left over. This money was just about enough to feed his newly acquired taste for speculating.

His new project would be one that would take a few years to come into fruition – it was no overnight get-rich-quick scheme - but, if he were careful, Jason reckoned that over five to six years he could probably triple his money or better.

The purchase went through smoothly enough. The executors of the old lady who had died were only too pleased to liquidate her principal asset and the whole process was completed in a couple of months. He moved in a week later.

The removal van had had to park across a shared drive to unload the relatively few personal possessions that he had allowed himself to bring. Less than five minutes after it had parked, Jason was met by a young man who somewhat stiffly introduced himself as his new neighbour before asking how long the drive would be blocked for. Jason immediately took the opportunity to tell him where to go and what to do when he got there – just in case the man was in any doubt. Jason's strong words and his large physical presence had not been what his neighbour had been expecting and he had beaten a hasty retreat indoors, muttering about 'consideration'.

Since then, Jason had planted Leylandii to block the sunlight from his neighbour's house, had held loud parties that were not quite raucous enough to get him an ASBO, and left his wheelie bin open as near to his neighbour's kitchen window as possible so that they were plagued with flies. Also, and knowing how his neighbour felt about blocking the drive, Jason had abandoned his Mercedes diagonally across it at every opportunity.

Not that the neighbours on the other side were exempt, either. Jason had hacked back their mature fruit tree where it ventured over the property line into his garden, making sure to coat the cut ends generously with herbicide, set up halogen security lights that shone directly into their bedroom window, lit bonfires whenever the wind was blowing in their direction, and so on.

The odd solicitor's letter arrived asking him to desist but, as Jason well knew, he was doing nothing illegal and he carried on heedless of their thinly veiled threats. This continued for some months until eventually, the mainly elderly people and young families living in the little group of houses, formed a residents group to discuss Jason and what to do about him. They had also elected a representative, one of whose functions was to explain the group's grievances to the perpetrator in person.

Jason had, so far, only received one visit from this representative who had tried to verbalise the little group's demands before being suddenly silenced by an expletive and a door slamming in his face. The occasion only served to convince Jason that he was on the home stretch and that success lay just around the corner.

The neighbours with whom he shared a drive were the first to go. One day Jason returned home to see that the house next door was empty and that a 'For Sale' sign had been erected in the garden. A quick call to the estate agents established that the owners had moved into a hotel and also that they were demanding the full normal asking price. You can dream on, Jason thought to himself.

A short while later, and after the expenditure of a mere couple of hundred pounds which he considered a true bargain, Jason was the proud possessor of two light-coloured cars that had clearly been involved in fatal or near fatal road accidents. He had an extremely inquisitive tow-truck driver place the hulks as near to the empty house as he dared.

Another trip to a theatrical agent supplied him with several litres of imitation 'stage' blood. This he spread liberally over the dashboards around the broken windows (one he had to smash a bit further) and over the seats and doors. He had to admit it looked truly gruesome when he had finished. Maybe he could rent the set out to a road safety organisation when he'd finished, he thought wickedly.

He also collected some very rusty engine parts, bald tyres, and various bits of exhaust from a scrap dealer who was only too pleased to see the back of stuff that had no chance of selling. These pieces he liberally scattered over the lawn.

Late one night, using only the moon for illumination, he dug a small pit in his neighbour's garden in which he laid some concrete inspection pit sections. He then emptied a sack-full of bones and inedible offal that he had got from a local butcher into the chamber before placing an ill-fitting manhole cover over the top, and tidying the soil around it. Now it looked like an authentic part of the drainage system, he decided. It would also stink to high heaven once it had had time to fester a bit.

After the appointed estate agent had taken a few potential buyers around the property, Jason made his move. None of the visits had lasted more than a few minutes and one family had not even bothered getting out of their car to look in detail. Jason had watched their horrified faces with amusement through his grimy front room window. He wished that he had a camera with a telephoto lens to hand.

After this last fruitless visit, he decided to make the young and harassed agent an offer he hoped the lad would not be able to refuse – so to speak. Jason put in an offer for a third of the asking price with the private promise that, if the agent could persuade the owners to accept what was likely to be the only bid they would receive, Jason would discuss sole agency rights concerning the ambitious plans that he had for the row of houses.

The agent had to work extremely hard to persuade the owners to accept. Their mortgage was well in excess of what Jason was offering, but as the agent pointed out, with Jason living next door, they were not going to realise any equity on the property therefore what difference did it make what he paid? Let the mortgage company pick up the tab. Making a loss or breaking even – either way made no difference. Best to just get out before it got worse.

Jason's offer was therefore grudgingly accepted and he now turned his attention to the family which lived two doors away. In order to make himself and his intentions 'better known', he knocked through to his new purchase and recommenced his war of attrition.

It soon became obvious to the owners of the other houses that it was just a question of time before they were targeted and, although they tried to get Jason arrested or, at the very least, restrained, he was always careful to not be seen to be doing anything illegal. Yes, the police and council officers privately agreed, he was a bad neighbour, but not a nuisance by the legal definition and therefore they could not act against him.

Over the next eighteen months, Jason bought up all of the other houses except one that was owned by an elderly lady who had dwelt there since she was a child. She lived alone and had only her aging dog for company.

Since her hearing was poor, Jason's loud parties or his 'working' late on his wrecked cars was singularly pointless. Making her financial offers was meaningless – she just wasn't interested - and his normal aggressive intimidatory tactics were too risky to use against an old lady who might drop dead as a result. If that happened, there was a police sergeant who had visited his house on more than one occasion because of the complaints, and who would be very interested. He would just love the opportunity to arrest Jason for something like manslaughter. No, it was a chance he couldn't take - he had to find another way of shoe-horning the old girl out of her home.

In the end, he came up with a plan. An unpleasant evening spent with a scoop and polythene bag in the dog walk area of one of the local parks, netted him a good supply of pooch-poo which he spread liberally around the old lady's front garden in the middle of the night. He just hoped no-one did DNA tests on it because then they'd know it wasn't her mutt. The idea made him laugh. He also scattered old newspapers, magazines, empty boxes, and various other items of rubbish on her lawn.

Finally, he made an anonymous call to Social Services telling them that he had been driving past one night and had been forced to stop by an old lady clad only in a stinking night dress who was wandering around in the middle of the road. He told them how she seemed very confused and kept asking when the next bus left for town. He laid it on with a trowel about how concerned he was for the old lady's safety. Being the public-spirited individual he was, he told them how he had parked his car and guided the old lady back to her home which, he couldn't help but notice, stank even worse than she did. Next time she might not be so lucky.

A few days later, a female Social Services representative arrived. Gingerly picking her way through the foul-smelling and untidy garden, the bespectacled young lady was not long in deciding that the house's occupant would be much better off in sheltered accommodation. The property was put on the market and Jason snapped it up after a tip-off from the agent.

Jason now had what he wanted and he was finally able to get his plans drawn up for demolishing these ugly boxes. In order to sell it to the Planning Department, the dangerous bend would be widened out by acceleration and deceleration lanes and a bell-mouthed road would lead from the apex of the corner to a new estate of what were euphemistically called 'executive homes'.

These attractive little boxes would have tiny, bathroom-mat sized lawns and gardens, and, in order to boost their value, come complete with a garage – a box that was marginally wider than an average car. 'Cram 'em in' thought Jason as he played with his calculator for the umpteenth time.

The architect had done a good job. The plans looked perfect and more or less as Jason had envisaged five years and several hundred thousand pounds previously. He just needed to get the forms to apply for planning permission and then submit the package for their approval. He couldn't see anyone objecting – after all, there was no-one there to object. He laughed aloud and toasted his forthcoming success.

The next morning, the postman reluctantly struggled past the various mountains of wrecked cars, stinking manholes, hacked trees and paper-strewn lawns to deliver the essentially identical recorded delivery letter to each house. Jason was dragged from a pleasant night's sleep full of dreams about sports cars and scantily clad female admirers to sign for his copy. Puzzled and worried, he signed for the other envelopes, too.

The letter was from the local council. Sometime back, they had seen an opportunity to finally get something done about the dangerous bend that had been responsible for too many deaths and horrific injuries over the years. The principal obstacle to its improvement had been the outcry that would have gone up from the owners of the houses when their front gardens turned into asphalt and crash barrier. However now, and thanks to Jason, the residents had all gone – apart from one.

Since the properties had now become officially derelict, the land they occupied could be correspondingly downgraded. This meant that any Compulsory Purchase Order the council issued could be accompanied by a much lower compensatory payment than when the homes had been habitable. Their plans to widen the road and improve visibility which had for so long been shelved, could finally be implemented.

Jason was looking at one of these Compulsory Purchase Orders. Ripping open the other envelopes, he quickly discovered that each of his properties was about to lose most of its front garden and, in each case, he would receive only minimal compensation since the land had been downgraded. Worse still, the loss of land rendered the construction of the executive homes only borderline profitable, even if the council did approve his plans which, to add insult to injury, he would now have to pay the architect to modify.

The only chance Jason would realistically have of ridding himself of these houses without making a loss would be to clear all the rubbish from the gardens and renovate the properties. If he was very, very lucky and managed to find people who didn't mind living so close to the main road, he would not lose too much on the deal.

HOBSON'S CHOICE

Part 1

August 15, 1971

"Daddy! I need to do a wee-wee! I think Benji does as well!" piped a shrill voice from the back seat of the car.

It was fair comment. It had, indeed, been a long journey for an impatient 5-year old and a wappy Dalmatian puppy but they would soon be at their destination, a holiday cottage that was virtually on the beach.

In order to make the journey as relatively stress-free as possible, Roger, his wife Melanie and their daughter Jessie had set off in the small hours and travelled through the night. They were now on the final stretch of newly-built motorway, a couple of junctions before their exit which in turn was a relatively short trip through country lanes to the sea.

"We'll soon be there, sweetie," Roger calmly assured his daughter, "won't we, Mel?" he continued, turning to his wife. "You've been doing the navigating, how much further do you reckon? We can't stop on the motorway though, Jess, or the Police will be cross with us."

"But I need to go!" Jessie wailed.

"Can you hold on for a bit, Jessie?" pleaded Mel. "It'll only be a few more ..."

Melanie's words were interrupted by a shuddering from the front near-side wheel. It was followed by a lurch to the same side, causing Mel and Jessie to jump in their seats. Roger immediately slowed. The car slithered on the damp asphalt of the motorway.

"Blast! I think we've got a flat and a bad one, too. I'm going to have to pull over and have a look." As he said this, Roger steered the vehicle onto the hard shoulder. Seeing what looked like some broken windscreen glass glistening some way in front of them, he brought the car to a sudden stop, jolting all of them. "Sorry. Didn't want to get a second flat-we've only got the one spare tyre."

"I thought the Police would be cross if we stopped here, Daddy," Jessie pointed out with the irritating logic of a five-year-old.

"It's OK if it's for an emergency, sweetie."

"But my wee-wee was an emergency, Daddy."

"Ye-es, well you two stay here and I'll get out and have a look." Roger was glad of the opportunity to remove himself from a discussion which he could not hope to win. Let Mel handle, it, he thought guiltily.

He turned on his hazard lights on and checked in the mirrors that there were no cars immediately behind him, then, closing his door behind him, went round to the front passenger side next to where his wife was sitting. She was watching him through the window with that encouraging but hopeless smile which she wore on all such occasions. She loved him dearly but knew with complete confidence that he was mechanically incompetent and would need the help of a friendly passing motorist to carry out such a complex thing as changing a tyre.

Roger read her thoughts-he'd seen that look too many times before. Well, this time, he was going to prove her wrong. He'd been reading up in the manual about how to perform odd 'car things' like checking the oil and water, adding anti-freeze and, praise-be, changing tyres.

He would certainly have to change it. You didn't need to be a mechanic to see that the tyre was flat-it was right down to the rim. Just as well he had stopped when he had; it might have been dangerous otherwise.

Roger Pearce, 35, assistant accountant, given to gangliness and thinning hair, was the proud possessor of two left hands. The only problem was that he was right-handed. He stooped over the hatch, behind which lay the spare wheel and also the puppy they had bought to grow up with Jessie. Given the difficulties that Mel had had in childbirth and the high probability that Jessie would remain an only child, they had agreed that a dog would be a good companion for their daughter. The two of them had certainly bonded.

"Stay, Benji. Stay!" Roger commanded. The Dalmatian pricked his ears at his master's voice and came to attention. He got up off his haunches and went into the sit position. "Good boy, good boy," Roger praised him, opening the hatch of their lime-green Austin Maxi.

Whatever caught Benji's eyes, ears or nose was not clear but he catapulted from his place in the hatch with such force that his front paws touched ground half-way across the inside lane. From there he bolted across their side of the motorway, which thankfully was not busy at that time of the morning, before leaping over the crash barrier that bordered their carriageway. There was a quick glimpse of his back legs and an excited howl before he disappeared head-first into the undergrowth. Even if Roger had been prepared, there was little he could have done to prevent him from making a run for it.

"Benji!!!" screamed Jessie, pushing open the door with all her strength and leaping out of the car. Without a thought, she, too, raced across their carriageway and was at the crash barrier before either Melanie or Roger could say or do anything. Roger gave a silent prayer of thanks that she had been lucky-there had been no traffic at the instant she had made her headlong dash and, like Benji, she had been unbelievably quick off the blocks. Jessie was now leaning over the barrier, frantically looking for any sign of her errant pet in the bushes and nettles beyond.

Roger was desperate with worry.

"Stay EXACTLY where you are, sweetie," he called out to her from his place on the hard shoulder. "Whatever happens don't move unless Daddy tells you too. I want you to face that metal thing and hold on to it as tightly as you can!"

There was no sign that Jessie had heard. She had her back turned and was presumably too fixated on locating Benji to pay attention.

"Jessie! It's important you listen to me! Do exactly as I say. Do you understand me?" He shouted as loud as he could. This time she seemed to hear but he couldn't be entirely sure.

There was a roar as a car went past at well over 70 miles an hour, taking advantage of the quiet motorway, no doubt. As it did, Melanie jumped out of their car, screaming incoherently, her long blonde hair flying across her face and into her mouth. She ran to where Roger was standing.

There was a muffled sob and a stifled "Yes", from Jessie. She was clearly and quite rightly very scared.

Fortunately it was the other carriageway that was busier-the traffic consisting mainly of early-morning commuters heading towards the town they had just passed. Hopefully, it would not be difficult to find a gap in the intermittent flow of vehicles.

"Melanie! Melanie!," Roger shook his wife in an uncharacteristically violent manner until she looked into his eyes. "Leave this to me, please. You'll only confuse her."

Melanie stopped screaming and began to sob.

Part 2 A

Several vehicles passed and, although there probably would have been no difficulty in finding a gap big enough for Jessie to run back to the car, with Melanie looking on and Jessie herself in a state of semi-shock, Roger felt it best to wait for a much bigger lull in traffic. Again, luck was on their side as no-one was using the outside lane next to where Jessie was clinging.

Finally, there was a major break in the traffic. In fact, Roger could see no other cars for a long way back. Jessie could make it easily and with plenty of time to spare.

Roger shouted, "Right Jessie, I want you to run towards me as fast as you can!"

"I want Benji!" Jessie wailed.

"Just run NOW!!!!" Roger shouted with a vehemence that surprised himself.

Jessie ran across the road, her stubby little legs flying. Melanie had her arms outstretched, urging her daughter on. Just as she was about to be gathered up by her mother, there was a high-pitched howl from the other carriageway rapidly followed by a 'Bdmmm Bdmmm' sound.

"Benji!!!!" Jessie shouted, turning and running back towards the central reservation.

By this time the opening in the traffic had gone by and a car was closing fast, its driver focussed on the journey ahead and completely oblivious of the young child in the road.

It was too late. Only at the last moment did the driver spot the child in front of him. There was a screech as he hit the brakes with all the force he could muster but it was too late to prevent the collision and there was a sickening thud followed by an ear-piercing shriek as Jessica was tossed over the bonnet and against the windscreen where her head shattered the glass. Finally, what was left of her dying and bloody torso performed a somersault over the roof of the car.

The scream was the last sound she would ever make.

Part 2 B

A car went flying past and then several more together. It crossed Roger's mind to take a chance and get Jessie to just run back to them but Melanie was already in such a state, that the last thing he needed was to cause her to completely lose it. He was also worried about Jessie's preoccupation with locating Benji.

When, at last, he saw a clear opening in the traffic, he raced across the three lanes of glistening asphalt, for once actually thankful for his long legs. He was so pleased to clamp his arms around his young and very frightened daughter that he couldn't resist shouting joyously back to Melanie, "Got her!"

Roger didn't hear her reply because suddenly there was another string of traffic. He held on tightly to Jessie's right-hand and sheltered her with his body against the crash barrier.

"I want Benji, Daddy. Where's Benji?" Jessie demanded through her tears.

"I expect he's found a rabbit or something. Let's very quickly call him but whatever happens we can't stay here, Jessie. Mummy needs us back at the car."

Roger took a deep breath; that blasted dog, he thought. "Benji! Benji" he shouted.

More traffic was coming including a slow moving vehicle which was hogging the middle lane even though there was nothing in the inside lane. The driver of the car behind, no doubt irritated by the thoughtlessness of the action, started to overtake.

It was at exactly that moment that Benji appeared. Probably scared witless by the noise, the calling of his name and the prospect of being abandoned, he bounded past Jessie and Roger and across the road and right into the path of the car in the middle lane. As he did so, Jessie, in a spontaneous movement, reached out with her free hand to grab him; thus taking half of her torso into the path of the faster-moving car in the outside lane.

There were two sickening thumps as Benji was crushed beneath the wheels of the car in the middle lane. A fraction of a second later Jessie's hand was snatched out of Roger's with such force that he later found out that he had dislocated his shoulder. Her head collided with the car's wing mirror and her arm caught its door handle which together span her small body around like a paper bag in the breeze. It did a pirouette through the air as if chasing after the car before eventually being slammed into the crash barrier some ten metres further up the road. The force of the impact caused her spine to be smashed, her spleen ruptured and her brain damaged irreparably. It could have been considered a mercy when she died a few minutes later.

Part 2 C

Grabbing his torch from the boot, Roger ran some twenty metres back down the hard shoulder. He stood as near to the edge of the carriageway as he dared, flashing his torch on and off at the windscreens of passing vehicles, jumping up and down and frantically waving his hands.

Several cars drove past, some of the drivers staring at

him-confused by this strange man and his torch. There was one car hogging the middle lane and another one overtaking it. It was close for comfort and Roger was worried for Jessie's safety. He was pleased to see, though, that his daughter, no doubt scared out of her wits, had followed his instructions to the letter and was clinging tightly to the crash barrier.

Eventually a car stopped and put its hazard lights on, its driver nervously looking in the mirror. Another car behind, seeing the flashing lights, also slowed down. Both drivers turned to Roger for an explanation but then, seeing the little girl clutching the central barrier, exchanged their angry puzzled looks for ones of concern.

Roger had successfully managed to stop traffic in the nearside lane and there was a car slowing down in the middle lane, too. Not long now, he thought, crossing his fingers.

Several drivers further back in the nearside lane sounded their horns in irritation and, perhaps fortunately for everyone, this masked the sound of Benji's dying howl as he was run over on the other carriageway while pursuing a rabbit he had unearthed in the central reservation.

It was going to be OK. Roger could now safely venture into the inside and middle lanes in order to slow down and stop any traffic in the outside lane. Unfortunately behind the slowing car in the middle lane was an articulated lorry travelling much too fast to stop in time. The driver, seeing Roger in the middle lane, realised in the split second that he had to think about it, that if he hit the car in front, that would mow Roger down. As a result, he slewed across into the fast lane, slamming on his air-brakes as he did. The noise of a thousand banshees on heat filled the air, deafening Roger.

The lorry's trailer shot outwards as a result of the sudden change in direction. It hit the crash barrier with such force that it dislodged Jessie's hold further down the barrier, throwing her directly back into the path of the lorry. The bumper smashed into her chest, caving in her ribs which, a micro-second later, pierced her lungs. Her body was then thrown head-first into the asphalt, smashing in her skull and causing instantaneous death. Her lifeless body was then dragged the length of the truck and trailer before its bloody fragments were scattered out behind.

Roger could hear Melanie's hysterical screaming above the shrieking of metal and the blaring of horns.

Part 3

August 16, 1971

An article appeared in the local paper:

There was a fatal crash on the motorway in the early hours of yesterday morning when Jessie Pearce, five-year-old daughter of Roger and Melanie Pearce, was run over while attempting to recover the family's pet dog. Their car, driven by Mr Pearce, had stopped on the hard shoulder following a puncture. Jessie had then apparently been allowed to get out of the vehicle and cross to the central reservation. The Police are now interviewing the father, a 35-year-old accountant, about how his daughter came to be on the motorway. The family dog was also killed in the accident.

To this reporter, it would appear that Mr Pearce made the wrong choice when attempting to rescue his daughter.

DEAR JOHN

It wasn't exactly writer's block; that wasn't it. It was just that she couldn't quite decide where the novel she was working on would go next.

Anne Bolson was midway through finishing her second book and she was having terminal problems with the plot. The heroine was stuck in a loveless marriage and now wanted out. Unfortunately she didn't have the courage to tell her husband to his face because she was afraid that he would persuade her to stay and then she would never escape. The only logical answer seemed to be to make a quick disappearance——maybe she should leave a typical 'Dear John' note first, though.

The trouble was that Anne couldn't quite decide how her heroine's partner would respond to the note. Would he be angry, depressed or just indifferent? Maybe he would be pleased and take the opportunity to start afresh like his soon-to-be ex-wife. Anne couldn't make up her mind and her agent was pressuring her for something concrete to give to the agency's proof readers.

At the seat of the problem was that Anne had no real

notion of what being trapped in an unhappy marriage was like. Fortunately for her, the book was pure fiction and in no way autobiographical. In real life, Anne was a few years younger than her heroine and she was also happily married-to Tony. They had been together six years now and, although they had agreed to start trying to conceive, were still childless. The truth was that Anne didn't really want any young children running around the house and demanding her attention while she was getting a career as a writer off the ground. As a result, she had been surreptitiously taking birth control tablets.

Sitting at the breakfast table one morning after Tony had left for work and before she had started clearing the bowls and cutlery away, Anne suddenly hit on an idea that would resolve her writing problem. However, in order to make it work, she would need the help of her best friend, Liz, whose home was a few houses along on the upwardly-mobile estate where they both lived. She gave Liz a quick call and asked her over for coffee on the pretext that it was a writing break.

Liz was the same age as Anne and they had been at school together some ten years earlier. Liz, always the tom-boyish brunette with the slight figure, had worked her way through a steady progression of both jobs and boyfriends, conspicuously and carefully keeping herself childless in the hope that Mr Right was just around the corner. She was currently in-between boyfriends and, so she proudly stated, in-between jobs, too.

A few minutes later Liz arrived. She was wearing her favourite red bib and brace outfit with an old tee-shirt underneath. Anne knew it would bear some faded protest slogan-her friend was always looking for new causes or underdogs to champion. Liz's garb contrasted completely with Anne's lace-trimmed full skirt and fussy peach-coloured blouse but then perhaps that was why they got on so well together-the 'chalk and cheese' girls as they had been called at school.

"Liz, I'm having terrible problems with this damned novel," Anne announced as she poured dark, aromatic coffee from a ceramic jug. They were sitting at the kitchen table that, despite its exorbitant cost, she had insisted on buying to match the newly-installed units. Its price-tag had made Tony squirm at the time but Anne had wanted a homogenous designer look and she had won the day. Now, leaning over its fine-grained surface, she smiled coyly at her friend and raked the carefully-manicured fingers of her right hand through her long blonde hair.

"I might have guessed," Liz sighed. This wasn't exactly a surprise, after all. "Every time I sneak a peek over your shoulder you're on the same chapter. What's the matter?"

"When you and your latest ex split up, did you ever contemplate writing him a 'Dear John' letter and then doing a moonlit flit?" Anne looked up from her coffee and met Liz's eyes. This was the crux of her problem and she wanted to fully gauge her friend's reaction.

"If I had, I would have rammed it down his lying throat," Liz exclaimed, half-angry, half-amused at the thought. "No, I think it's fair to say that if we had had that level of communication, we might have stayed together."

"I'm being serious, Liz." Glib comments weren't going to help her sort this out. "I'm stuck. I can't work out what reaction I should get my main man to display when his ever-loving walks out on him." She paused for a moment. Liz thankfully stayed quiet allowing her to finish. "If I go by the films, he will go off the rails and be inconsolable with grief however I reckon that's just Hollywood's view of things and not real life." She tipped the remnants of her coffee into Tony's cup and poured herself another from the percolator. Liz declined a fill-up.

"So, what do you suggest? Is there no way around it? Can't they just have a big row?"

"Not really, and for much the same reason as you and your ex didn't leave notes for each other."

"Presumably you can't finish the book if you don't sort it out."

"No, and I've now got my agent on my back, too." Anne sipped her scalding hot coffee. The steam wafted past her eyes making them water slightly.

"Have you an idea? I'm guessing that's why you invited me over during your work time that's supposed to be so sacrosanct."

"We-ell, yes, I do," Anne replaced her coffee cup and moved it around in front of her, "I'm going to need your help, though."

"What would you like me to do?" Liz asked suspiciously.

"I'm going to set Tony up with a 'Dear John' letter to see how he will react. I know it's weird but I need to do this research for my novel." She paused for dramatic effect and to see how the idea was registering on her friend. "I want you to be around so that you can tell me afterwards how he took the news. I'd also like you to let him in on the surprise before he does anything rash. You'll need to sort the timing out for that." She paused again, took a deep breath and smiled. "I trust your judgement. Can you do that for me?"

Liz looked startled. "I, uh, I don't know. This really is a lot to ask, Anne. Are you absolutely sure about it?"

"Yes. I've thought it through and I'm sure Tony will see the funny side afterwards and ..." deep breath, fingers crossed, "... it'll be just what I need to finish this damned book. I'll make it up to him."

There was silence for a moment.

"Well, OK but I have reservations. Still, if your mind's made up, who am I to argue?" Liz added the last phrase with a smile.

The next day, Tony came home from work to find a letter:

Dear Tony

I'm sorry to tell you that I have left you. I can't stand it any more and I need to get away. I hope you will remember the time we have spent together with great fondness as I certainly do. Please do not come looking for me. I will let Liz know when I am settled and she can arrange for my things to be sent on.

Please look after yourself.

Anne

There was a knock on the door and Tony opened it to see Liz standing on the doorstep. She was grinning widely. Tony ushered her into the living room where he had opened a bottle of Mateus Rosé he had picked up from an off-licence on the way home.

"I can't believe she'd do this," Tony exclaimed,

fetching two large crystal glasses from the sideboard. He poured out the pink liquid and handed Liz her drink.

"Well, that's the line you were supposed to use …" Liz said laughing. She reached up and gave Tony a long and lingering French kiss. "… although I'm not sure this was the outcome she was anticipating," she breathed over him as their lips parted.

They both laughed so loudly that they were afraid somebody would hear.

"The hard thing to do was to get her to delete the line which said that she hadn't found anyone else."

"No, that wouldn't have done, would it?" Tony grinned at how quickly Liz had sized up the situation. That decisiveness was one of many things he loved about her- you wouldn't catch her spending week after week wondering about what should happen next in a stupid story nor would she take her contraceptive pills on the quiet hoping you wouldn't find out.

"I'm fed up with sitting on the sidelines watching her not appreciate what she's got. Are you ready for the next bit? Then we can be properly together and not have to share everything with her."

"Definitely. I've had a gutful of that precious writing of hers. It's so much more damned important than 'us'."

"OK, well if you're ready then," she paused a moment, "here goes." Liz picked up the new 'no-contract' mobile phone she had paid cash for at a large electrical department store. As far as she could see, it was the only real weak link in the chain but it was unlikely that anyone would be able to trace the phone back to her. If there were no robberies at the store, the security camera video tapes would be recorded over in a few weeks and then it would just be down to a vague memory from a disinterested shop assistant. It was an acceptable risk.

Liz dialled Anne's phone.

"Hello, who is this?" Anne asked cautiously, not recognising the number on the display.

"It's me. I had to borrow a friend's mobile as I dropped mine in the sink this morning. That's not important, though. I need to speak to you urgently," Liz said, trying to sound frantic while Tony distracted her by massaging her neck. It always turned her on, damn him. She pulled away slightly from him-now was not the time to lose concentration.

"What's up?" There was a note of panic in Anne's voice.

"Well, I'm not sure about Tony. I wouldn't say he's gone off the rails but he's very badly depressed. I know the experiment is important to you so I'm not asking you to come home now but I do need to speak to you about him and exactly what we tell him and when. I've given him something else other than you to think about for the moment but I must see you about him and soon."

"Can't we talk now?"

"No, it's – one minute – yes, look I can't discuss it with you now, please make sure it is delivered next week, will you?" A short pause followed, "Sorry, Anne, Tony was in earshot. I've settled him down and tried to give him a bit of reassurance without giving the game away"

"Thanks, Liz, you're a pal."

"Right, but we still need to meet up, pronto. Can you get to the supermarket car park? Somewhere at the back? About nine o'clock?"

"Um, yes, I suppose so. It's not terribly convenient but I can do it if you think it's important."

"It is. Must go now. Bye," Liz abruptly disconnected and immediately turned the phone off.

"We mustn't take the phone with us because they can trace where it goes and we need to destroy it as soon as we can," Liz said firmly. "Get the stuff together and then we'll be ready to leave. I've made us a picnic dinner so that there aren't two sets of dirty plates."

"You've thought of everything, I'm so proud of you, darling," Tony beamed.

"I'm just fed up with playing second fiddle to her-she doesn't appreciate you."

"I know," Tony sighed, "I didn't realise just how lonely and miserable I was until we got together."

Just before nine o'clock, Liz was ready and waiting in the car park. Shortly afterwards, Anne's red Alfa Romeo turned into the entrance and rolled slowly over to where her friend was parked. She turned off the ignition, looked cautiously around to see if Tony was in attendance, and then climbed out. She walked over to where Liz was leaning against the bonnet of her own car.

"So, what's up with Tony?" Anne asked sharply, "You've got me all worried."

"I need you to come and have a look at this," Liz took her over to the car's open boot.

"There's nothing in here. What am I supposed to …?" the question remained unfinished as Tony suddenly appeared from his hiding place on the far side of the car. He leapt on top of Anne from behind while Liz swivelled her round so that her head was resting on the inside of the boot. Tony had wrapped his hand firmly across her mouth. He was wearing thick leather gloves as Liz had told him to- just in case Anne tried to bite. It wouldn't do to be having to explain why he had a fresh bite-mark that exactly matched the dental profile of his wife's teeth.

Liz calmly produced an old washing-up bottle that she had sent through the dishwasher a number of times first. Inside the bottle was a cocktail of Anne's medicines that Liz had found on the shelf in the bathroom. Liz had carefully crushed the tablets on some newspaper, poured the powder into the bottle and then added a generous amount of brandy to mix it with. She had worn gloves the whole time, wiped the brandy bottle clean (just in case) and had burnt the old newspaper in a small hole in the garden which she later backfilled with soil.

Tony removed his hand on cue and Liz rammed a plastic funnel into Anne's mouth serving to stifle her friend's scream so that it came out as a muted gurgle. With Tony using his weight and strength to subdue the struggling Anne, Liz squirted the mixture into the funnel and down Anne's throat.

"How long do you think it will take to work?" Tony asked nervously.

"It's impossible to say but it was a hell of a dose I gave her," Liz said, clearly shaking from the effort and the occasion, "Just don't let go of her, will you?"

"No, of course not."

They checked Anne's pulse several times and, when they were satisfied that it had stopped, they carried the body back to the Alfa and settled her into the driving seat. Liz then deliberately spilt the brandy over Anne's clothes and the car's upholstery before putting the now nearly empty bottle into the dead hand and allowing it to slip to the floor. She scattered the empty pill bottles alongside it.

"Let's get home, now, darling," she smiled, taking his arm as if they were on a country walk. "You need to be phoning the Police soon. Don't forget you're a very worried husband."

"I know," he gently squeezed her arm with his free hand, "and I could sure have used some of that brandy, I can tell you."

"Later," Liz promised, flashing him one of her sexiest smiles. She threw her head back making her curly hair shine even in the gloom, "I'll console you, don't you worry."

A few moments later, Tony was back at their house and phoning the Police. When he shyly told them about the 'Dear John' note that had left for him, their disinterest rapidly turned to poorly-disguised mockery. They're going to have to eat those words, thought Tony mischievously, still now was not the time to point out their erroneous assumptions.

Much later that night, two officers from the local CID arrived on his doorstep. Tony pretended to have been half-asleep on the sofa although he had actually been trying to concentrate on a TV film. It had proved difficult with both what was going through his head and also the muted sound. The officers calmly and concisely broke the news to him that his wife had been found dead, comforted him as he feigned shock and surprise and then asked to see the letter that had been left for him.

One of the officers, the more senior one, took the note, read it and then placed it in a small polythene evidence bag, carefully recording the time, date and place.

"I have to say, sir, this does resemble a classic suicide." he said, matter-of-factly. "The lady seemingly took an overdose and washed it down with some very strong drink. She was dead on arrival at the hospital. Your note very conveniently ties it all together which does make our lives a lot easier. Normally, and when you felt up to it, we'd ask you to come down to the station to answer a few questions about your relationship-you know, was she depressed or seeing anyone else, etc. It'd just be for the record, you understand."

Tony was about to respond when he stopped himself——there had been a slight note in the policeman's voice that didn't quite feel right. "I don't understand, officer, you said 'normally'. Look, this has come as a big shock to me and I'm not thinking clearly. Please explain," Tony tried to sound as subdued as possible.

"Well, I confess I'm no handwriting specialist but you see I've got two pieces of paper that would appear to come from the same pad. One of these notes was found at the scene and one presented to us by you. That makes me think that your wife probably wrote both of them. That would be a reasonable assumption, would you not think?"

"Um, yes, officer but I'm not sure what you mean by

that," Tony asked nervously. This wasn't part of the script and he had no idea what was going on or where it was leading.

"We always make a point of going through the deceased's belongings-you never know what you might find. Anyway," he said, pausing and clearly savouring the moment. He coughed, "Ahem, anyway, as I was saying, we found a letter in her handbag addressed to you. If you don't mind, and seeing as it's now evidence, I'll read it for you, sir. That only seems fair to me," he paused again as he fished out another and larger evidence bag from his pocket. He peered through the polythene. He read:

Dear Tony

I'm sorry to have done this to you but I needed to do research on relationships for my damned book. I now realise how stupid I have been and how much damage I may have done to you and us. Please forgive me. I am meeting Liz in a few minutes-she has known about my idea from the start but I swore her to secrecy so please don't blame her-and I intend to come back later tonight after we have spoken. I don't want to spend any more time away from you and I miss you terribly by the way.

All my love

Anne

"As I said, sir, I'm not one of them smart psychiatrist fellows, but that doesn't sound like a suicide note to me. Obviously you know your wife, so what do you think?"

"I couldn't say, officer, I'm still in shock."

"Now that makes perfect sense to me, sir. A chap whose just found out his wife has committed suicide is bound to be in shock-that's why we've already had a brief talk with this lady, Liz, about your wife's death. I found her number stored on your wife's mobile so that was convenient, wasn't it? Turns out this Liz says we should talk to you. So, here we are."

"I don't know what to say, officers," Tony was shaking and he was sure the sound was coming out in his voice.

"Well, let's not worry about that here, sir, you can think about that while you're benefiting from the five-star accommodation that Her Majesty is happy to provide free of charge for deserving causes. Read him his rights and cuff him, constable," he said, turning to the young officer.

"Good try," the officer whispered in Tony's ear.

EVERY ONE A WINNER

It was a series of events which Eric Whitelaw would not normally have remembered. Well, maybe he would have kept them in his head for a few days, but then they would have been completely forgotten. The events in question, though, were to completely change his life forever, and he was never to forget them.

It was a wet and dismal Tuesday in November. The rain seemed as grey as the asphalt pavement that it was splashing on, and it appeared to Eric that the whole world was just a myriad of shades of this colour. As normal, the children were late for school, his wife of fifteen years, Mary, had not quite finished preparing his lunchbox (those canteen lunches are so expensive and bad for your waistline, dear) and the dog was barking at nothing in particular in their narrow hallway.

Finally, Mary, a sensible wife if ever there was one – cheerful, buxom, plain-faced but with a ready smile, dark-but-greying hair, dressed in her usual 'January Sales' bargains - handed him his Tupperware lunchbox, kissed him on the cheek and pushed him to the door. He was already late, but if he hurried, he should still make the bus.

On the doorstep of the semi-detached house that they had struggled so hard to buy when they had first married, Eric turned to smile at Mary and say a quick goodbye to their two children, neither of whom was listening. Just as he did so, Puzzle, their 5-year-old Labrador cross, ran out into the garden and off down the pavement barking wildly. Eric chased after him and finally managed to catch up with him just before he entered a neighbour's garden in pursuit of their cat.

"You're going back to the house," Eric snapped at Puzzle, grabbing his collar and dragging the reluctant dog back to their home.

Having satisfied himself that Puzzle was not going to escape again, Eric raced off to get the bus that would take him to his job in the accounts department of a large DIY store.

The wind was driving the rain into his face and Eric could barely see where he was going. This, and the episode with Puzzle, delayed him enough so that he got into sight of the bus stop just in time to see the bus departing. The next one would be along in about twenty minutes and it would still get him to work on time – just – but he liked to get to work early and settle himself in with a cup of coffee before starting. Now he'd arrive flustered and would have to wait for break time.

The bus-stop was merely a lighting column with a bus

timetable and sign attached to it. There was no protection from the downpour and twenty minutes of standing there would have drenched him to the skin. Partly out of a need to shelter from the weather, and partly for a reason he would never be able to adequately explain, he went into a newsagent and lingered over the DIY magazines until he felt that decency require him to make a purchase.

Not wishing to spend three to five pounds on a magazine, Eric bought a packet of mints and, then on impulse, two lottery tickets on which he marked off the first numbers that came into his head.

"Why not have a go?" he thought, "you never know."

By the actual time of the draw, Eric had completely forgotten about the tickets. One of his children had caught a cold from the lousy winter weather, no doubt, and the other was looking like he was set to follow. If the lottery draw was on the television, it was on in the background and no-one was paying any attention to it.

In fact he forgot all about the tickets until the next day when there was a loud and purposeful knock on the door and Mary, rushing to answer with just her old house-coat on, was met with a man and a woman dressed in smart-expensive gear. They were both smiling sublimely at her.

It turned out that Eric's refuge from the elements and his spur-of-the-moment purchase had just won the Whitelaw family a cool fifteen million pounds.

Two months later, and after an extended holiday at their favourite hotel in Torremolinos, the Whitelaw family were home. Although they still struggled to believe their good fortune, they had taken the opportunity to relax and discuss the implications of their windfall.

They had also endured the interminable financial counselling of the various advisors supplied to them by the lottery organisation. Being of cautious disposition, the family had decided that they would each allow themselves one luxury and then put the rest into a savings scheme from which they would draw as necessary.

All had agreed that they did not wish to move from their home and Eric had surprisingly announced that he wanted to stay on at work in the DIY shop – at least for the time being. His reasoning was that he enjoyed his job and, with the lottery money behind him, there was no longer any pressure on him to be promoted so he could drop out of the rat-race which he so despised.

Mary's dream had been to completely and professionally redecorate the house, so over the next few weeks, a steady stream of interior designers, decorators and workmen traipsed in and out of the house.

The children, who had opposed any move which would mean them being separated from their friends, were allowed to buy a selection of gadgets and goodies that made them the envy of their peers, and Eric placed an order for the Aston Martin that he had always dreamt of.

They had returned home to a fanfare of photographers, journalists and local residents. Some were clearly jealous, but most people congratulated them and wished them well. Finally, after the hubbub had died down, they were left alone.

The difficulties started a few weeks after their return. Their pet dog, Puzzle, who had stayed with relatives while they were in Torremolinos, suddenly became violently sick. A trip to the vet and a thorough examination suggested that he had eaten tainted meat. He would recover but it left both Eric and Mary feeling uneasy. Not being able to pinpoint anything specific, they chose to say nothing about their fears to the children.

The day after Eric's Aston arrived, he bounded down the stairs, and making the excuse that he wanted to 'check something', ran out to admire his new car. It sat on his newly-resurfaced drive, gleaming in the Spring sunshine.

It was only when Eric walked around to the passenger side that he noticed that someone had made a deep scratch along the side of the car – presumably with their car key. This was no accident; it was a deliberate act of malice, and although the motive was presumably jealousy, Eric could not conceive of the mentality behind such an action.

A few more weeks passed uneventfully. The pointed jokes at work gradually wore thin, and the children's friends were only interested in helping them try out their collection of gizmos.

The circle of mothers that Mary belonged to admired the many changes she had made to the family nest, and contented themselves by making countless suggestions for further improvements as they nibbled the fancy biscuits and other delicacies she served them. If they had been asked, the Whitelaw family would have said that staying put was definitely the right decision. They were 'at home' in all senses of the phrase.

To Eric's private delight, Mary suddenly began taking an interest in her looks. Although still ferociously frugal, she had her hair done at an upmarket salon and she also joined a local health club. Not wanting to be alone, she graciously paid the full subscription for her two closest friends, and the three of them giggled their way through the range of sports and relaxation services on offer.

After a few weeks of going regularly, she looked much younger, and declared that she felt better than she had done in years. Eric was enormously proud to take her out for dinner, driving to La Madeleine, an expensive local restaurant, in his new Aston, while the children played computer games with the best babysitter they could find. Eric felt like James Bond with one of his supermodel double-agents beside him, and he mentally practiced saying "The name's Whitelaw. Eric Whitelaw."

Coming back from one such Friday night jaunt, Eric was surprised to see that their streetlight had gone out. It was not until after Mary phoned the Council on the Monday and a couple of workmen had attended, that Eric realised that the light had been shot out - probably by an air rifle.

He still had no clues as to who the perpetrator or perpetrators were. Of course there had been a number of snide comments from some locals, but they didn't amount to anything, really. Some people are only jealous, he told himself.

His answer came one Saturday morning when Mary was hanging clothes out on the washing line in their carefully tended but tiny back garden. She couldn't quite be sure what was being said but she was certain the remarks coming from the other side of the garden fence were far from friendly. The words sounded like thinly-disguised threats to her and the children but, as she couldn't be exactly sure, she kept it to herself even though it badly unnerved her.

The full and open declaration of hatred came when Eric returned from work to find his neighbour's car parked across the Whitelaw drive. Eric gingerly squeezed the huge Aston into a tiny space on the main road, walked back and knocked on his neighbour's door. After a few seconds, it opened and a man with a red face appeared. The man made no noise – he just stared angrily at Eric.

"Hello Jim. Look your car is parked across the end of my drive. Do us a favour, mate, and move it will you?"

There was no answer, just a glare. He decided to persevere, ignoring Jim's stony silence. "You can always put it back afterwards if you must. I shan't be going out again until work tomorrow morning." Eric said the words quietly and conscious of wishing to be seen to be firm but friendly.

"Why don't you and your family naff off somewhere? What you want to stay around here for?"

Eric was shocked, Jim's reaction had taken him completely unawares.

"We don't need you lording it up over us. Now get!" and, with that, Jim slammed the door in Eric's face.

The first time he was blocked out of his drive Eric did nothing, leaving the Aston parked on the main road under a streetlight that was now regularly being shot out – this latter fact being much to the annoyance of the local council. After a few such occasions when he was either prevented from parking on his drive or leaving for work, he called the Police.

A less than sympathetic constable came out, told him with a sneer that he didn't own the Public Highway, and that there was nothing that he could or would do. Why didn't Eric ask the neighbour nicely? He emphasised the word 'nicely'. There was a very clear underlying message that if Eric attempted to physically 'persuade' Jim to move his car he would be in trouble with 'The Law' for creating a disturbance. This blatant unfairness greatly irked the normally passive Eric.

Eric guessed that it was also Jim who sneaked around the outside house at night, filling their wheelie-bin with festering rubbish. Later, in the summer, he would have noisy barbeques until very late at night, and would very obviously take especially great delight when the wind direction caused the smoke to be blown back towards the Whitelaws' house.

Jim was also doing everything he could to make Eric and Mary's twice-weekly trips to their local pub as uncomfortable as possible. The odious man and his gaggle of cronies spent a large part of their spare time in the pub lounge, and whenever Eric and Mary came in, they would go into a huddle. There would then follow a host of sub-aural jibes resulting in much cheering or laughter.

In short, Jim did everything he could to drive the Whitelaw family from their home. Any tolerable existence was becoming impossible, and although they were otherwise very happy where they were, moving seemed to be the only answer. Eric and Mary sat up until late into the night discussing their options.

Not long after this discussion, one Thursday early in Autumn, Jim and his half-dozen mates were in the pub, busily knocking back their half-priced 'Happy Hour' drinks. Jim was a forty-something with a swelling beer-belly, hair that was starting to thin and, although he would never admit it, an unhappy home life. Like his friends he was a braggart, and it was a standard game for them to wind each other up with increasingly tall tales. Jim was mid-way through one of these anecdotes of dubious veracity when the whole pub went silent.

Jim turned his head in irritation to see what it was that had taken everyone's attention away from his latest boast. His eyes feasted on a tall blonde girl in her mid-twenties wearing a very minimalist designer mini-dress. While it covered 'the essentials' it also revealed just enough to hint at the treasures that lay beneath. She was pure sex-appeal, and Jim was instantly besotted with her.

The girl walked across the bar, pulled up a seat beside the group of men, turned towards them, smiled and said in a gentle but confident voice, "Hi." Having ordered a Rusty Nail which she sipped through her full, flame-red lips, she swivelled around on the chair showing an impossible amount of leg.

"I've heard that Eric Whitelaw, the lottery winner, comes in here. Is that right," she purred. "I'm Melanie, by the way".

"I live next door to him," Jim offered, pushing his way to the fore of his mates who were tongue-tied – talking to a woman like this was not the same as talking about one.

"I could tell you all about him. Know him well, I do. He's not a nice guy, though." He turned and smirked at his friends. "Unlike me," he added with a lascivious grin.

"I'd love to hear all about it," Melanie purred at him. "Why don't we sit over there?" She gestured to a free table, "It'll be much more private."

Jim tried hard to find some witty words but couldn't, so he tamely followed Melanie's legs and tight bottom over to the table. She unselfconsciously crossed her legs just like he'd seen Sharon Stone do in that film. He wondered if Melanie was wearing panties – he couldn't quite see.

Half an hour later, Melanie announced that she was ravenously hungry.

"I saw a restaurant called La Madeleine on the way here, it looked nice. What's it like?" Melanie asked Jim.

"Um, well, I've never, um been in there. It's supposed to be nice," he said awkwardly.

The Madeleine was a very, very expensive and sniffy French restaurant. He had once, in a rush of blood, thought about taking his wife there to celebrate their anniversary. Taking a quick and embarrassing recce trip, the prices had nearly knocked him senseless. The landlord of the Bull's Head, where they were now, had finally put on a bit of a spread for them at a fraction of the price and his wife was none the wiser. Unlike this girl, she wouldn't have appreciated the difference, anyway.

"Wonderful, I've really enjoyed our chat. Why don't you join me? I'd understand of course if you and your friends have other plans," Melanie asked him, flashing him another one of her dazzling smiles.

"I'd um love to but it's a bit …"

"It would be my treat. Really, I'd love it if you could come."

"OK, OK, yes, I'll just get my jacket," Jim spluttered, getting up so fast that he nearly knocked the table over.

Jim winked at the lads as he went past them. Whatever happened from here on in, this was going to be a yarn that he could tell and embroider for years to come. He snatched up his jacket and headed off after Melanie's shapely pins.

Her hot hatch was parked outside and Jim clambered in. God knows what the missus would say if she knew. He'd have to say he'd had too many pickled eggs and bags of crisps if she asked him why he didn't want his dinner. He'd also need to do something about Melanie's expensive perfume lingering on his clothes. That was a problem for later, he decided. This was the moment of a lifetime and not to be passed up because of the danger presented by his wife's nostrils.

When they arrived, Melanie had a quick word with the maître'd and they were shown to a very private table for two. She seemed thoroughly at home. She clearly understood the indecipherable menu, ingenuously translating it for his benefit, and then picked out a wine costing more per bottle than the whole of Jim's weekly supermarket shop. Not only that, she laughed at all his jokes and anecdotes. He felt dizzy but completely at ease.

Drifting back to Melanie's four-star hotel room seemed completely natural. By that time, Jim was light-headed from the wine and bursting with confidence. Melanie made him feel like he hadn't done in more years than he could remember – maybe better about himself than he'd ever felt.

She undressed, teasing him by strutting her beautifully fit and firm body in front of him, just out of reach of his greedy clutches. She seemed unbothered by his beer-belly and the knobbly knees that his wife regularly delighted in pointing out just as he dared to suggest sex. Melanie was both beautiful and game for things that he had only ever read about in the magazines that he and his friends passed around when they thought no-one was looking.

He was sitting up in bed admiring Melanie's breasts when the door opened. Eric and Mary stood in the doorway holding a state-of-the-art digital video camera, pointing it directly at them. To his further confusion, Melanie gave the Whitelaws a cheery wave.

"Smile for the camera, please," said Eric.

"What are you doing here?" Jim shouted, frantically reaching for trousers and underwear that Melanie had deliberately placed out of his immediate reach.

"I'm very impressed, Melanie. I don't know how you stomached it but you've earned every penny. I hope my wife won't mind if I include a little bonus." Eric looked at Mary who nodded and smiled, then handed Melanie a brown envelope while Jim scuttled around the room holding a white sheet over his abdomen. Mary carried on filming.

"Get your clothes on, Jim," said Eric icily. "Then we're going to talk. Or, rather, I'm going to talk and you're going to listen."

A few minutes later, Melanie had dressed, thanked Eric and Mary again and left. As soon as he heard the sound of her twin exhausts, Eric turned to Jim.

"You've three choices, Jim. I want you to think very, very carefully." He paused for effect.

"Choice one, you can move out of the neighbourhood. Choice two, you can start behaving like a good neighbour. Choice three, we upload this video onto Youtube so that your wife and anyone else who's interested can enjoy watching you star in your very own video. I would also invest in a professional website promoter to make sure that it got seen by as many people as possible."

Jim's face was ashen. He couldn't meet Eric's eyes and clearly didn't know what to say.

"The choice is entirely yours," Eric concluded. He transfixed Jim with his gaze while Mary continued recording their victory.

Jim muttered something completely indecipherable and looked down at his feet, but they didn't have any answers for him.

LUCKY CHARM

Robert3, so-named because he was the second generation clone from the original Robert, now long-since recycled, woke up sweating from the nightmare which regularly haunted him. The trouble was that the grey dawn light did nothing to dispel his terrors. When it came down to it, he just wasn't ready to die yet - it was that simple.

Just about very aspect of life on Earth in the 24th century had become regularised, and the compulsory cloning process which had been introduced a century before had gone a long way towards achieving that goal. With a population of 8 billion, the planet was already cracking at the seams. It just couldn't support any more humans.

With the exception of those who had been officially awarded the status of 'Contributor to the Human Race' (more affectionately known as 'Greybeards'), no-one over the age of 50 now existed on Earth. Procreation took place by cloning and this was conducted between the ages of 18 and 32 in order to allow the child time with his or her 'parent'.

Unfortunately Robert3 was now 49 years old and unwilling to face the compulsory euthanasia that was to be his fate unless he should die in the meantime. What a cheering thought. For this reason, he was also extremely jealous of Robert4, his twenty-year-old cloned 'brother'.

Of course, he always chose to emigrate to one of the Lunar or Martian outposts but he shuddered at that idea. It was rumoured that their virtual abandonment, because of the resources required to support them, had resorted in unspeakably unsavoury practices including incest and cannibalism.

Apart from the odd prison transport that went there, sending conventional rockets was now restricted to important matters such as uploading satellites for Ultranet – the worldwide network of computers, transport and all powered machinery ranging from the humble food processor upwards.

It was no good looking to outer space to help him avoid euthanasia. Following the explosion of the nuclear-powered Photon shuttle over Florida that rendered a large chunk of the state uninhabitable, efforts at exploring space had diminished, and Earth had become introspective. Its global government now just concerned itself with stopping population growth and marshalling its dwindling natural resources.

Robert3's thoughts were interrupted by an irritatingly whiney call from the kitchen.

"You forgot to order any cornflakes, brother."

Robert3 dressed quickly and went into the kitchen where Robert4 was polishing off the rest of the box. His clone's comment really meant that there were enough cornflakes for him but not for his parent. That was typical. Robert3 picked up the empty box and stuffed it in the recycling bin.

"Didn't think you'd mind," Robert4 said, spluttering the last of his breakfast across the table before dropping his spoon loudly in the empty bowl. "I must get off to the university pronto. I'm working on something really important. I'll see you later." Without waiting for an answer, he rushed out of the door.

"Don't worry, I'll just have coffee and clean up your mess," Robert3 muttered quietly to himself. If he'd said it too loudly, the automated housekeeping system might have taken it upon itself to kick in with all the chaos that usually resulted. It had been perfectly OK until a young Robert4 had hacked and reprogrammed it. But then he was born to be a hacker just like himself.

One of the key contributory factors to the compulsory euthanasia of 'mature' clones had been the studies carried out into the psychology of getting large masses of people to accept their fate without excessive resistance. The Holocaust during the Second World War; the numerous plane, ship and train hijackings; the various ethnic clearances of the 22nd century, had been carried out by a relatively few ruthless and despotic individuals on large groups of people who (for the most part) were led like lambs to the slaughter. Not that lambs now existed outside of pet farms, and even if they had, the Animal Rights faction would have gone berserk at the idea of their slaughter. Robert3 assumed that his failure to placidly accept his own predestined fate was probably down to the same free-thinking gene that had sent him down the path of becoming a computer hacker.

It was one of those occupations that officially didn't

exist. Hacking was either a social or civil crime depending upon who the target was. Paradoxically, there wasn't a single corporate entity which didn't indulge in it. You just couldn't carry on a business of any size without knowing what the competition was up to and then putting a large spanner in their works when the opportunity arose.

Robert3 scratched his scalp through his greying hair – his dandruff was bad again and he really should stop wearing dark suits until it had been treated. The brain was working underneath, though, and an idea was forming about how to avoid a star role during the annual 'Day of Rest' ceremony.

He went into Robert4's bedroom. It was the inevitable disarray of used clothes and half-soiled bed linen. A woman's touch would have made all the difference but Robert3's partner had given up on his extended working hours and the lengthy furtive conferences during which the holographic video screen would be switched off and the volume control manually set to 'earphones only'.

Such discussions might take place at any time of day or night and, finally, disgusted at the constant intrusions and the complete lack of attention from Robert3, she had left him for a clerk who worked in a vehicle registration office. The new guy's work schedule meant that he could give her the time and attention that Robert3 couldn't. She had taken her own clone with her and he had been left with the choice of either looking after Robert4 or having him assigned to an adopting family which had lost one or both of their own clones.

On top of the dressing table that now served Robert4 as a workbench, were scattered bits of computer, scraps of paper, and broken pencils. Suddenly his eyes hit on Robert4's identity bracelet. All of Earth's 8 billion citizens were supposed to wear this whenever they left the house. It contained not just the individual's medical history, education, work experience and credit history, but also a full record of where they had been and where they were authorised to go. Robert4, with his usual haphazard attitude towards anything outside of his immediate interest, had left it behind.

Robert3 could not wear this bracelet and then pretend to be Robert4 because one of the many thumbprint and retina scans would betray him. He didn't want to spend the rest of his relatively few days in a high-security prison convicted of identity theft. That didn't mean that he couldn't make use of his find, though.

Snatching up the bracelet, he ran into his own bedroom, and using the small port that allowed the police to verify a holder's identity, he connected it to a box that he produced from his drawer. A few seconds later the box had broken through the gadget's multiple firewalls and downloaded the bracelet's information. Having done this, he hastily replaced the bracelet where he had found it, shut the bedroom door, and scampered back to the kitchen just in time to see the front door open and Robert4 enter.

"Forgot my bracelet – the car wouldn't start," he offered by way of explanation.

"Easily done. I do it all the time," Robert3 replied, hoping that he wasn't betraying himself. His cloned brother was not paying attention – he was too busy searching his room for the missing article.

"Ah, there you are. I must have put you down when I brushed my hair."

The hair in question was blonde and streaked with red

as was the fashion for many of the youth. For some reason, it mattered a great deal. While Robert4's attire, posture and personality were all 'take it or leave it', his hair always   had   to   be   'just   so'.

Robert3 worked for one of the mega-corporations that now more or less controlled Earth's economy. Unfortunately, from their perspective, they didn't have a monopoly – it was a desire for this that he was trying to play on.

His regular nightmare and general trepidation about what the 'Day of Rest' would mean to him had been going on a long time, as had his plans for dealing with it. With that in mind, some twelve months ago, he had presented himself in front of the chairman – a feat that had taken some doing with the chairman only consenting to the appointment because of Robert3's impeccable service record.

They had had a brief but very enlightening conversation and it had gone much better than Robert3 had dared to hope. The old man (as chairman he was deemed one of the Greybeards – a status which meant that he was allowed to live to his natural expiry date) desperately wanted to recruit one of their competitor's top researchers but, if he did, there would be all sorts of legal ramifications as a host of laws would be broken in the process.

The identity bracelet of the researcher would simply be placed in front of a judge and this would show the individual's full employment record – absolute proof that he had compromised his company's confidentiality and restrictive employment clauses. Not only that, Robert3's corporation would be deemed equally culpable and fined a not-so-small fortune.

But, of course, if this specific bracelet could be 'adjusted' then the case would fall apart. The researcher's former employer might even end up being sued for making slanderous allegations. That would just be the icing on the cake.

The only difficulty with 'adjusting' the bracelet was its heavy duty encryption software. This stuff was cutting edge, multi-layered and absolutely tamper-proof. If that wasn't enough, anyone foolishly attempting to make changes to the data it contained would find themselves facing a bevy of armed police in well under five minutes. As a result, playing around with one was quite out of the question.

The chairman had the answer. Refusing to make much by way of a comment, he had produced a handful of bracelets belonging to clones who had 'retired' the previous year. On their demise, the bracelets had been deactivated and ordered for secure destruction. One of the chairman's undercover men had obviously intercepted them en route.

This gave Robert3 the means to access, at his leisure and in complete safety, an inactive and unregistered bracelet.

With many hours of careful investigation, testing, and adjusting behind him, Robert3 was as confident as he could be that it was possible to copy the data from an active bracelet to an expired one and then change some of the data on the copied version.

While visibly continuing his ongoing top secret work for the chairman, he allowed himself time to edit the copy of his clone's data from the little box so that the associated retina scan and fingerprint were now his, while all other details remained that of his clone. It wouldn't pay to make too many changes. Having done this he transferred the data to one of the defunct bracelets which he then dropped casually in his briefcase. Being deactivated, the bracelet fortunately didn't set off his office's security system. He was ready.

On the eve of his 'Day of Rest', Robert3, spent several hours with beauticians and hairdressers. This wasn't that unusual – many soon-to-be-retired clones saw no merit in hanging on to their savings and blew it on 'looking their best for the executioner'.

Robert3 had the works done. That involved everything from injections of nano-bots to lift his face, to the micro-repairing of his split ends. By the time he left, it had taken years off him and visibly depleted his bank balance.

He had arranged to spend that evening with his clone getting quietly and slowly drunk. It was to be a private farewell celebration unlike the public festivities that were being conducted outside of their apartment. It was an anathema to Robert3 how so many supposedly intelligent people could so placidly accept their forthcoming destruction.

"Well, brother, I shall miss you – you know that," Robert4 said glibly in a feeble attempt to behave comfortingly.

"I wish I could say likewise," Robert3 joked. "I can tell you one thing, though, your turn will come sooner than you realise."

"I don't think about it – it's all a long way off."

"Yes, of course. Let me get the beers – you stay there."

Robert3 came in with two huge glasses brimming with ice-cold frothy beer. Since it had been a very warm summer day, they were both suitably thirsty and supped the ale enthusiastically.

"Groove the locks – looks dead cool. Don't you fancy a few hours with some high-class tail on your last night?" Robert4 asked.

"I thought I'd rather spend the time with you – we both seem to have been preoccupied with our careers lately."

"Yeah, well, no disrespect but if it were me, I'd be doing some serious thinking with my trousers right now." Robert4 patted his crotch and took a long swig from his glass.

"Have you any plans to settle down?" Robert3 queried.

"Um, no, I don't … You know this is strong beer. Where did you, um … where did …" and with that he fell over, the remaining beer spreading rapidly across the tiles. Robert3 heard the automated cleaning system readying itself.

"No! Cleaning Off!" he shouted. The last thing he needed now was the farcical situation that the automated system would undoubtedly create.

Robert3 slung his clone over his shoulder and took him into the bedroom.

"'m OK, really," Robert4 burbled before letting rip a

deafeningly loud snore.

Having laid him down on the bed, Robert3 removed his clone's bracelet, replaced it with his own, and left the room.

If anyone carefully examined the bracelet, they would immediately see that the encryption was of a style not exactly consistent with Robert4's presumed age, but that was a chance he would just have to take. In reality, the inspectors didn't look for that kind of thing. All they wanted was a corresponding body and bracelet for each name on their round-up list. These were jaded people who, over the years, had heard just about every reason for people not wanting to attend the Day of Rest.

Now, all he had to do was to make his clone look the part.

A visit a few weeks back to a nearby theatrical store had located some 'Quickage' as they called it. Applied as a facial cream, it made the face muscles sag a bit and the skin appear blotchy and veined. The effect was intended for movie shoots or plays and would wear off within 48 hours. The hairdresser-beautician he had visited had also, and somewhat reluctantly, supplied him with a greying solution that would change the colour of any hair it was applied to.

The drug he had given his clone should last until the lethal injections were being applied and that was all that mattered. Despite numerous requests from the public to have the actual deaths televised, the authorities had steadfastly refused to do so. Robert3 privately suspected that the placid bovine-like acceptance wore off for most people when they were being strapped in a chair ready for the syringe bearing their name. Such a display wouldn't be the sort of thing that was in the public interest.

A few hours later, Robert4 looked at least 20 years older than he actually was. It wasn't really enough but it would have to do. The point was that he didn't look his true age.

There had been a public outcry about 'Big Brother' when the bracelets were first introduced (the idea that the government would be able to monitor bedroom and bathroom activities was generally abhorrent to most people) and so a 'deactivation' button had been fitted. While it was perfectly legal to deactivate the bracelet while you were in your own home, do it outside or leave it behind and you were in deep water. Put it this way – you only did it the once.

He deactivated his clone's original bracelet and put it in his pocket, ready to dispose of later in the block's incinerator. The bracelet he had stolen from work was still in his briefcase so he went over to it, took it out and put it on. Robert3 slept better that night than he had done in a long time.

The next morning, Robert4 was still sound asleep when there was a very businesslike knock on the door. Robert3 opened it to see two burly armed guards, poised, their arms crossed. One spoke.

"Robert3 Wilkins is required to come with us. Is that you?" he droned – it was clearly a dreary task that he was well accustomed to.

"No, he's in his room. He got very drunk last night. Sorry, I was with him – I probably should have told him to ease off," Robert3 apologised.

"No problem. A lot of them do that. I'd rather haul a drunk one to the van than go chasing after a runner," the guard chuckled. He is human after all, thought Robert3.

The two guards went into Robert4's bedroom. Robert3 heard a muffled, "What d'y' want?" but they didn't reply. One of them lifted up Robert4's bracelet arm, scanned it and announced, "That's him. Come on, let's get him in the van."

Robert4 was beginning to come around a bit now and was protesting more coherently.

The guard who had until now remained silent said, "You are Robert3 Wilkins and you are due to attend the Day of Rest ceremony."

"I'm not Robert3, I'm Robert4. You got the wrong person. Tell him brother," he appealed to his clone.

"I'm sorry he's giving you so many problems, he's been fine about it until now. I just hope when it's my turn I can go with a bit more dignity." Robert3 turned towards his clone and smiled. "Goodbye brother – I wish you well."

"You bastar…" He didn't finish because the second guard had slapped a muffler over his face and was bundling him into the collection van.

He had done it. Barring some last minute disaster he had bought himself another 30 years. Who knows what he could do in the meantime or what it would be like then. It wouldn't do to be too callous but he intended to party a bit and generally celebrate his reprieve.

Robert3 or Robert4, as his bracelet now declared him to be, was still in a euphoric mood when there was another knock. Smiling contentedly, he opened the door. He was met by two more armed guards. It must be a mistake, he thought.

"Robert3's gone, I'm afraid. Two guards have already taken him," Robert3/4 told them.

Ignoring him, the guard asked, "Robert4 Wilkins?"

"Ye-es, that's me," Robert answered with a little trepidation. What on earth was this all about?

One of the guards roughly seized his arm, scanned the bracelet, and nodded. The other guard droned:

"You have been charged, tried, and convicted in absentia for attempted crimes against the State in that you did wilfully attempt to hack into the Revenue Services network with a view to committing an act of fraud. Your sentence is that you shall be assigned to either a Martian or Lunar work colony for thirty years or until you shall die of natural causes, whichever shall be sooner."

The guard paused. Rober3/4 was dumbstruck. He opened his mouth but no words came out. The guard, meanwhile, drew a deep breath and then continued:

"Since you have hitherto had a clean record, the judges have generously consented that you may express a preference as to which colony you shall be assigned to. You have seven days within which to do that otherwise a choice will be made for you. Do you understand?"

"But, I … um, didn't do anything. Really, I didn't."

"I'm sorry, sir, but I'm not here to debate the issue. You may, of course, engage an advocate while you are in detention on Earth but you should be advised that all your possessions are forfeit in order to pay for your accommodation and transportation." He turned to the second guard, "Take him to the vehicle," he rapped.

THE RACING LINE

It was common knowledge that some of the pit mechanics were claiming to have seen strange shadowy figures wandering around. None of the drivers had, though, and, with the casual aloofness that tended to go hand-in-hand with the motor-racing elite, they collectively dismissed these sightings as being the result of their crews inhaling too many exotic fumes.

Mad Tony, aka Antonio Moretti from Dorenza, had his mind on other things – namely the art of winning at all costs, a single-minded objective which propelled him to take the risks that had given rise to his nickname. At the age of twenty-five he was in his prime, already the champion of several of this year's Grand Prix's, and much-pursued by the flocks of stunningly attractive young ladies that frequented the circuits.

Besides his prowess behind the wheel, Tony was also fortunate enough to be blessed by rugged masculine good looks. His black hair was just long enough to be deemed rebellious yet short enough to not be considered effeminate. His piercing blue eyes and his seductive smile only further served to increase his magnetic effect on the female sex.

Unlike with many other sports, being of slightly below average height like Tony was, served as a real boon when it came to getting into your car. His diminutive stature also encouraged the more mature female disciples to mother him. In other words, Tony was a real 'Golden Boy'.

His admiration society wasn't just restricted to female membership. The team's mechanics and manager benefited immensely from the success that accompanied him although, if you could have investigated the darker recesses of their minds, you might well have found that they were harbouring dark feelings of envy over the many extravagant trappings he took for granted.

Today Tony was at his home circuit in Dorenza, a modest-sized town in the Lombardy region in the north of Italy. As a result, he was extra keen to win and, if as was likely to prove necessary, he had every intention of living up to his nickname in order to achieve that goal.

He strutted confidently across the pit road, waving to the fans who had arrived early in order to watch him do his practice laps and get his autograph if they were lucky. He entered the pit which had been assigned to him and his team, and where the two chief mechanics were busily putting the finishing touches to his car.

The younger one of the two mechanics, Fabio, a wiry and muscular lad not much his junior, was reaching for the engine cover – hopefully with a view to it being replaced, Tony thought, chewing his lip in irritation. Until the tuning-up had been done and the cover put back on, he would have to wait to take the car out on the track. Then, and only then, could he do the practice laps which would dictate his place on the starting grid.

"I tell you, boss, I ain't the only one who sees these creatures. Two of the guys in the Ferrari pit have seen 'em, too. One of the Mercedes drivers reckons he heard them speaking English but with really weird voices. He thinks they're aliens."

"Don't be daft. You don't listen to him – he's just a dreamer," said Pierre, the no-nonsense French senior mechanic now speaking in his slightly stilted English, the more or less universal language of the pits.

"I don't believe in that stuff. It's just superstition put about by young mechanics that haven't got enough to do." Tony winked at Pierre. Winding up the youngsters was a popular second sport to the actual driving. "Is the car ready now?" He jabbed his finger in the direction of the partially-covered engine.

"Give me two minutes to wipe her down, start her up, and listen to her turn over. Then she's all yours," Fabio replied confidently, not rising to the bait. He put the engine cover loosely over the car, and stretched to his full height of five feet four. The machine was his pride and joy and he tended it as if it were his favourite but demanding progeny.

His expression suddenly became thoughtful.

"But they've seen 'em. Men, well, they say it could be men but they've got these weird things on their heads and they're completely covered from head to toe in suits of all different colours," he said handing Pierre the spanner he'd been using.

Neither Pierre nor Tony were listening. They were engrossed looking at some technical charts that Pierre had produced showing the circuit in terms of rpm and gear selection.

"I think we're being invaded by Martians," Fabio persisted, despite the complete lack of attention his remarks were receiving. Finally, realising Fabio wasn't about to 'button it', Pierre looked up from the charts, groaning inwardly at this particular scuttlebutt that was currently pervading the pits. That was the trouble with these youngsters, too much imagination and not enough action. You couldn't say that about Tony, mind - he was definitely not to be found lacking when it came to action.

Having finally got his audience to listen, Fabio went back to fitting the engine cover over its retaining bolts.

"There you go, boss," he said, tightening the last wing nut. "She'll go like the wind out there."

Tony climbed into his gleaming new car, and the two mechanics pushed him out to the where his pit joined with the pit lane. Starting up the engine, he looked carefully behind to see that there were no other cars about to run into him, and then pulled out onto the track, flooring the accelerator and making his engine scream in protest. His fans, who had been waiting in their grandstand seats for hours for just this moment, cheered and waved vigorously to him.

After all the other drivers had concluded their practice and timed laps, the grid order was finally established. To his dismay, Tony discovered that he was to be stationed a few rows back from pole position despite his crew's earlier assurances that his car was in tip-top condition. It didn't occur to him that the slight difference between his time and the fastest lap might be down to his own performance rather than that of the machine.

* _ * _ *

It was the day of the Grand Prix. The grandstand was full to capacity and all non-necessary personnel had been cleared from the circuit. The starter climbed his gantry and waited impatiently to give the order for the race to get underway.

Tony sat in his car, also twitching with the urge to get going, and reflecting on the general strategy that he had agreed with his team manager an hour or so beforehand. Like the other drivers in the front rows, he knew that if he could get into the lead early on, he would be able to avoid the mayhem that often occurred further back as the less experienced drivers and the lower specification vehicles struggled to keep up. This was a situation which often led to collisions, some of which could be fatal. He didn't want any part of that.

The idea was to get to and maintain second or third place for the first three-quarters of the race, biding his time in case the leader or leaders broke down. If this didn't happen, then, and when the opportunity arose, the home straight would be the preferred overtaking point. It was the only really long, wide section of the course and he would be able to push his car right to its limit in reasonable safety. It would also be directly in front of his supporters so that would be an added treat for them.

When the time for the race to begin had arrived, Fabio was firmly ushered back to the pits by the track marshals. Pierre gave his driver one last pat on the back before he, too, was sent running after Fabio. A few seconds later the official waved the chequered flag from his gantry and the race was finally underway.

Although he quickly made up a few places from his

starting position, Tony still found himself in third, unable to make any headway on the two in front and dogged in turn by a couple of drivers behind him. But this was just as he and the team manager had expected so he satisfied himself with biding his time all in accordance with their plan.

With two-thirds of the race gone, Tony decided to wait no longer and to make his move. He came off the bend leading to the home straight and gave the car its full head. His luck was in because the two cars in front of him, who were busy fighting it out with each other neck-and-neck and not looking behind, had drifted wide a second or two previously on the same corner thus losing them precious time. With a roar of his engine he raced through the gears and saw the ground between himself and the two leaders rapidly diminishing.

They only spotted Antonio as he came through between them: the discordant whine of the three protesting engines producing a deafening and continuous high-pitched shriek. Bit-by-bit he edged past them as both other drivers looked anxiously across at him. By the time he had reached the start line, he was in first place.

As he came into sight of the stand, his supporters, realising their hero was now leading the race, jumped up from their seats to wave and urge him on. In return, he injudiciously took one hand off the wheel in a show of regal bravado to gesture back to them. The home crowd loved it.

Just as he moved into the racing line position that he would need if he were to tackle the next corner in the most efficient manner, a figure suddenly appeared directly in his path. He or it was clad in a brightly-coloured one-piece suit and porting a strange dark-visored helmet - just like

Fabio had described. In the split second that Antonio had to react before the unavoidable collision, he observed that the creature seemed entirely oblivious to his presence and was making absolutely no attempt to get out of his way.

The spectators' roar died in their throats as their hero seemingly without reason swerved violently, lost control, and span around to face the oncoming second and third-placed cars. There was a high-pitched shriek from the brakes of these two other vehicles but the speeds and distance involved meant that there was only a token reduction in momentum before the unavoidable collision.

Tony's car hit the other two more or less simultaneously as he slewed sideways across the track. On impact, his vehicle's nose and tail became detached, rupturing the fuel tank which spontaneously ignited. An imperceptibly small split second later, it began spraying liquid fire over all three cars. Meanwhile, the angle at which his car had made contact was causing the second and third placed vehicles to collide nose-to-nose. Their front wheels struck each other before detaching, bouncing once or twice on the track and ricocheting off into the grandstand where they ploughed into four terrified onlookers.

Tony was instantly crushed to death, and the remnants of his vehicle ripped through the side of the second and third-placed cars, rupturing their fuel tanks and causing two enormous explosions a split second apart. A single blindingly-bright yellow fireball erupted from the still-moving wreckage, incinerating the other two drivers, and despatching scorching hot metal shards into the grandstand where they killed or maimed a number of spectators.

It could have been a lot worse but the pursuing drivers

were fortunately far enough behind the leaders to be able to slow down in time. If not, the death toll would probably have been a great deal higher.

＿＿*

Dave Moulton, Team Ferrari's new driver, stomped irritably across the track towards the Dorenza pit lane. His car had packed up coming down the home straight and he had left it parked next to the gantry near the start line. In a hurry to get away from the object of his anger and frustration, he had not stopped to remove his helmet and only did so as he neared the pit wall. For some reason, the air felt strangely cold, despite the June sunshine that beat down on his back. He shivered, and promised himself a hot shower and, in a very non-Italian way, a large steaming mug of coffee when he got back to his pit.

The sunlight glinted on a small brass plaque which he had hitherto never spotted, despite having raced at this particular track several times before. It was written in Italian, but having picked up a lot of the language from his Ferrari team-mates, he knew sufficient to understand its meaning.

It read:

> *"5th June 1911, killed in a tragic accident:*
>
> *Moretti, Antonio*
>
> *De Santis, Dino*
>
> *Manini, Alfonso*
>
> *and 11 spectators"*

That was exactly one hundred years to the day – a real

coincidence. But it happened a lot more then than nowadays because cars had got a lot safer. It didn't stop them from breaking down, though.

THE BENCH

"Come on Les, it's well gone 8 o'clock. Time to be moving on,"

The voice came from a tall, uniformed policeman who was bending over a seemingly formless pile of rags, polythene bags and newspapers that some non-civic-minded hooligan might thoughtlessly have strewn over a park bench.

The pile of rags stirred.

"Wha'ssup? 'Smy bench, find yer own," a gravelly voice came from under last week's newspapers.

"Up now, Les. You know the score. And don't forget to put those bottles in the bin." The policeman pointed at the two empty cider bottles underneath the bench.

"I ain't no litterbug. You knows that," Les said, surfacing from the various layers of insulation that he had wrapped around himself. It might be April but there was still a real nip in the air and he was feeling it more each year. He grabbed the papers and started stuffing them inside his clothing.

"Yeah, I know, Les, but I'm sticking my neck out letting you stay here as it is. My sergeant finds out and he'll have me checking parked cars for expired licences till Doomsday."

"'Swhy I dropped out. Too many so and so's trying to tell you what to do all the time," Les grumbled, lighting his first smoke of the day. It was one of his special composites made up of half-smoked cigarettes that had been discarded by people with 'more money than sense'.

Unabashedly scratching his crotch Les announced, "I need a Jimmy bad. See you," and he beetled quickly off towards the nearby Public Conveniences.

Neither the policeman, who went on to continue his early morning beat, nor Les, who was in urgent need of a place to dispose of the previous night's alcohol, noticed that a dirty green satchel had been left behind.

An hour or so later, two teenage boys who were supposed to be at school but who were playing their regular game of truant, found the satchel. They sat down on the bench and tipped it upside down in their search for 'cash, ciggies or drugs'. The quest was in vain and they only found a few photos, a Bible, and some faded letters which they threw towards the water.

"Chuck the bag, it stinks," one of the boys said, bored with the trophy.

"Get off that seat, a lady wants it," a monster of a man boomed at them, and the two boys skedaddled, throwing the satchel in the boating pond as they ran off laughing and turning over the rubbish bins.

"I'm sorry, I just can't take any more, Pat," Noreen, sobbed from behind her hands. She had settled herself on the bench that the boys had vacated.

Patrick grabbed at her but Noreen shrugged him off.

"It's too late for that. Your mistrust has completely killed this relationship. Everywhere I go, every man I speak to, you suspect of having an affair with me. I can't take it," there were more sobs from behind the fingers.

"It's just the way I am," Patrick said gruffly, "and you shouldn't make me so suspicious."

They made a strange pair, him over 6 feet high and her halfway between four and five feet tall. Despite that and all of Pat's plentiful testosterone, Noreen was finally getting together the confidence to call the shots.

Noreen was sitting at one end of the bench, crying into her hands and Pat at the other, periodically shaking his head and fuming at any passer-by he thought was mocking him.

"I can't marry someone who doesn't believe in me and trusts me implicitly," she finally said, uncovering her face. "I don't know who that person will be but it isn't you, Pat. Please take your ring back." Noreen started to remove it from her finger.

"You're mine!" Pat said from between clenched teeth, "You'll always be my girl."

"Please take your ring," Noreen repeated icily while trying to push the ring into one of his mallet-sized fists.

"I don't want the ring! We're going to get married!"

With that he jumped up from the bench and loomed over Noreen.

"Take your damned ring!" she spat, and threw it at him. Spontaneously he tried to catch it in mid-air but his huge hand merely batted it back towards Noreen. The ring sailed over her head and disappeared into the grass and leaves near the water's edge.

"I'm going now, Pat. Goodbye," and with that she got up off the bench and walked away.

"You'll regret it," Pat called after her, "and don't go coming back, neither." Then he added, "Cos I'm not having you."

A few minutes later, Pat was running after Noreen leaving the engagement ring where it lay.

William had brought his lunch which, as always, he had carefully made the night before in his one-room bachelor pad. He liked to call it that to his married friends who were convinced that he was constantly 'on the pull'. The terrible truth was that William (or Bill as he preferred to be known) was thirty and still a virgin. Not only that, he had not had a single date in over two years.

It wasn't that he was particularly ugly, nor was he overweight or scrawny. OK, his choice of clothes were from a fashion that had ceased being popular several years before (but why wear decent stuff to the office?) and, as a result, looked a little dull and shabby. Even William would admit that if pushed.

William's face tended to be a bit on the round side and his flesh was inclined to sagginess, but his principal handicap in the matrimonial stakes was his shyness. If he entered a room with girls of his age present, they would gradually drift away until only he was left. If he tried to make contact with a friendly-looking one, his verbal clumsiness meant that he would end up being either shunned or ignored. It made for a painful and embarrassing experience.

William now sat on the bench, intermittently munching his cheese and lettuce sandwich and feeding the myriad of assorted birds that came flocking towards him after they had had less fruitful forays on and around the boating pond.

He held out a particularly big piece of crust. A swan swiped its neck forward, attempting to grab the bread but, in doing so, knocking it clean out of William's hand and into the long grass by the edge of the path. The swan briefly sought it out but then, having been unsuccessful, gave up and strutted off huffily. Not wishing for the morsel to be wasted, William got down on the asphalt to look for it.

The bread had disintegrated into two halves and one of the halves was lying next to something gold – like gold foil. Those damned kids, littering again, he tutted to himself, but this was no piece of litter; it was a ring with a sparkling jewel in the middle. William picked it up and looked at it in more detail.

Somebody must be missing this, he thought to himself. Someone who's lucky enough to have another someone want them enough to ask them to get married, he considered glumly.

William wasn't a superstitious person – well, that's what he would have said if asked - but he avidly read the astrology column every day, stepped over cracks in the pavement, steadfastly avoided anything with 13 in it, and was a nervous wreck every time Friday 13th came up. Of course he would hand the ring in at the police station – that was the honest and correct thing to do - but the ring was an omen, too. Today, he decided, was the day he was going to start the process of finding someone who wanted him. He was sure of it - you just couldn't argue with fate.

Humming quietly to himself, William got up from the bench, brushed the crumbs off his ancient jacket, much to the delight of the gulls, sparrows and starlings, and headed off in the same direction that Noreen had gone several hours earlier.

Later that day, while trying to hand in the ring he met Noreen who was being passed from one policeman to another. She was there to make a formal complaint against Pat who had spent the whole day following her through town threatening both her and anyone she spoke to.

Noreen immediately identified the ring and this got her talking to William about its history. She was also glad of someone so clearly non-aggressive to talk to and her friendliness and William's conviction that 'today was the day', gave him the confidence to eventually ask her out on a date. It was 'just for a coffee', of course. Noreen accepted with a smile that had William clicking his heels with delight.

"Cor, I need to rest me old bones a mo'. Mind if we stop 'ere just for a quick break?" Lily, the self-appointed leader of the 'three friends' urged the aforementioned old bones to make one last supreme effort to get as far as the park bench.

Lily, Daisy and Emily - the 'E's - had a combined age of well over 200 and they were always keen to impart their acquired wisdom to anyone who gave the pretence of listening. They 'hung out' together (as Emily, the most modern-thinking one of them was apt to say), in a home for the elderly (but not quite insane, Lily joked) and would escape at every opportunity.

Daisy was the quiet planner who normally came up with the ideas for how to spend the day. Today it was a trip into town, a wander around the boating lake, and then back to the 'Old Folk's Home' for tea.

It was getting on in the afternoon now and darkness was not far off. Although there were three of them, privately they all feared the dark – the time of muggers, bag-snatchers, and worse. Tea-time at the Home was boringly predictable but at least - and more importantly these days - it was safe.

"I remember when this was just fields," Lily said, suddenly.

"No you don't," corrected Daisy, "You come from up North. You weren't here when they made all this."

"Lil' might not have been but I was," offered Emily attempting to keep the peace. "They wanted to put houses here but some big-wig put the boot in. I can't remember who it was but they had his name put on all the benches in his honour."

Emily turned to inspect the bench they were sitting on. "Yes, here it is, an inscription 'in memoriam' – there you go," she pointed at a small, time-darkened brass plate screwed to the back of the seat.

"Never noticed that before," exclaimed Lily, "Funny, innit, you live here all your life and you don't see something like that. Oh well," she sat down again and turned back to the other two ladies. "Who's up for bingo, tonight?"

From some way off, the two boys whom Pat had earlier sent packing, spotted the old ladies. One boy was in an empty shopping trolley which the other was pushing. They suddenly veered across to the bench, clearly looking for mischief. The three ladies bunched up together defensively.

"Wanna one-way trip to the cemetery, grannies?" the boy in the trolley demanded.

"Give us yer purses and we'll take yer there," the other boy shouted mockingly. In a show of bravado, he shoved his mate in the trolley towards the lake.

"Eh, what you doin'?" He jumped out just before the trolley splashed into the muddy water, scaring the ducks and swans into a burst of protest.

The boys started scrapping with each other and the three elderly ladies tacitly decided that now was a good time to be moving on. There was no point in tempting fate; modern youths had no respect and most of them were drug-crazed and carried knives – they had seen it on the telly and read about it in the papers.

Just as the boys were about to take off after the three women, they glimpsed the young policeman striding towards them. They certainly had no wish to enter into discussions with him. Apart from having made his acquaintance on prior occasions, the last thing they needed was him checking up on them and finding out that they had been skiving off school all day.

Abandoning the trolley, they legged it off in the direction of a little corner shop that was happy to sell them both individual cigarettes and cans of beer, and cider from a multi-pack, as long as they had the necessary cash and no-one was looking.

The policeman sighed at the sight of the trolley in the lake. He was just about to go off duty and had no desire to spend his own time locating the relevant supermarket manager, less still be seen pushing the trolley through the streets. If an amateur photographer should catch him doing that, copies of the picture would be pasted on the police station wall for years to come along with, no doubt, a whole variety of suitably 'witty' captions.

As he pondered, Les arrived from the opposite direction carrying his usual polythene bags which were chinking loudly with the 'medicinal anti-freeze' that got him through the colder parts of the night.

"Wha's up?" he asked, "By the way, you seen my satchel?"

"No, sorry, Les. In answer to your other question, look: some little toe-rag has pushed this trolley into the lake."

"Don't you worry about that; Les'll take care of it."

The tramp smiled, pushed the policeman aside and extracted the trolley from several inches of cold and sticky mud. He suddenly bent forward towards the reeds and exclaimed, "'Ere, I've found me satchel! Them soddin' kids must have had fun with it." Les was so pleased with himself that he nearly fell over backwards in his excitement.

He then searched around in the gathering dark for the

scattered contents of the bag, the policeman shining his powerful torch in front of him to help. They scoured the reed bed, with Les occasionally stopping to pick up a piece of paper which he inspected at length.

"Think I've got most of it," Les announced finally, "It's nuffin to anyone else but it's precious to me – photos of me family, and some important letters from them."

"We were very lucky, Les. If the park inspector had seen it first, he would have chucked it all. Anyway, what you going to do with the trolley? I can't let you leave it here."

"Nar, course not, I got me a mate who works at the supermarket. Gives me a fiver for every one I takes back."

Without saying another word, he shoved his bags and satchel into the trolley and set off towards the supermarket, whistling tunelessly through the gaps in his teeth. Just time to catch them before closing and, with any luck, the fiver might get turned into a bottle of cognac or malt whisky which had 'fallen off a rickety shelf'. That would be nice. Something a bit special to warm himself with as he settled down on his lucky bench.

A DAY AT THE BEACH

This was the second week of their family's summer holiday, and despite their fears of what might be, the weather had been benevolent so far.

"I think it's going to be another lovely day today, darling," Lorna winked to her husband, Colin, who had briefly looked up from stowing the awkwardly shaped camping gear into their car.

Colin simply smiled, shoved the heavy green canvas tent bag easily into the boot and then slammed the hatch down so hard that the whole car shook from the force. He was a man of relatively few words. Perhaps that was no bad thing, Lorna thought, given the nature of his work. The other thing she admired about him was that he was blessed with a fine physique helped by plenty of regular exercise.

Lorna found herself contemplating his ample biceps which were stretching the fabric of his checked cotton shirt to bursting point. There was no time and no place for bedroom action on a family camping holiday – she'd have to wait until they got home.

"C'mon kids, it's time to go!" she shouted at their 10-year-old twins, Daniel and Daphne, who were playing some game which only they understood involving a tennis ball, a football, and a stick. The kids dropped the stick and handed the balls to their father who grumbled, opened the hatch, stuffed them in beside the tent bag and then slammed the hatch down again, this time even harder than before.

They'd paid for the pitch in cash the night before so there was nothing left to do but strap everyone in and then drive off up the rough track that lead to the campsite's entrance.

"How far to the beach?" Colin asked suddenly as they were crossing the cattle grid and pulling out of the farmer's gate where they'd camped.

"Not far, hon. I think it's less than 10 miles." Lorna reached in the glove compartment for a map. She didn't like the way SatNav tracked your movements and that made her deeply suspicious of it. You knew where you were with a map, she thought, while laughing inwardly at her own joke. There wasn't much point in cracking it publicly as Colin might not get it straightaway and that would only anger him. The twins were too busy scrapping in the back to be impressed either.

About half an hour later, they arrived at the seaside. They'd deliberately restricted their 'on the beach' sessions to weekdays which, although still far from easy, at least made parking reasonably close to the sands a realistic possibility.

"There's a space, Dad!" Daniel shouted to his father, tapping him roughly on the shoulder and pointing enthusiastically towards a space which was just large enough for them to drive into forwards.

"I like ones at the end of a bay, Dan," Colin grunted.

"You remember, Daniel? Daddy doesn't like getting stuck in a tight space and, even though it's OK now, it may be chock-a-block when we come to leave."

"Umm, over there," Daniel pointed his finger at a space on the end of a line of parked cars. The double yellows began immediately beyond it and, unless someone with a disabled sticker parked on them, it would make for a guaranteed trouble-free egress.

"Well spotted, Daniel," Lorna praised her son.

In mock pride, Daniel smirked at his sister who then jabbed him hard in the ribs with her elbow. "Ow!" he yelled, and prodded her back twice with his. A fight was just about to break out in the back when Colin span his head around and shouted, "Enough!"

The twins knew better than to risk incurring their father's wrath so they instantly stopped scrapping. They looked sullen and crestfallen.

"Don't forget to wear your sunglasses and hats at all times," Lorna reminded them. "And I mean at all times".

"Even in the sea?" asked Daphne facetiously.

"You know that I come down to the sea with you and

hang on to them until you come out. Now, put those hats and glasses on and no more arguing," Lorna ordered.

They gathered up their beach kit, locked and alarmed the car, and then descended the steps onto the baking hot sand. It was the middle of the summer season and the sun was beating down, making them appreciate the straw hats that made them look like a squad of Oxford punters. There wasn't a cloud in the deep blue sky whose colour was only further enhanced by the wrap-around polarising sunglasses they also sported.

"Over there!" Lorna gestured urgently to a patch of sand adjacent to a middle-aged couple who were clearly being irritated by the proximity of a bunch of young lads playing football. Their ball was being kicked closer and closer to them and the husband looked much too puny and nervous to offer a viable deterrent.

Colin dropped the bags down in the spot Lorna had suggested, and then walked over to the young men. One of them, obviously the bravest, asked, "Wanna game?"

After a moment's hesitation, Colin replied, "Yeah, why not?"

With that, he picked up the ball and drop-kicked it with such force that it flew into the waves just beyond where they broke into a white froth. The first boy clenched his fists and turned sharply towards Colin, but a quick glance at Colin's expression, his unsettlingly obvious muscular frame, and the distance that the ball had travelled, made him refrain from any open hostility. Instead he yelled at the youngest boy in their group, "Go and get the ball!"

The lad in question sighed with obvious resignation to his fate and jogged down the beach to the water. The group's pecking order had clearly been well-established.

"Goodbye," said Colin, emphasising the word to extract the maximum menace from it. He turned back to his family.

The boys got the unambiguous message and traipsed off after their mate who, since the ball was slowly drifting in with the tide, was debating whether he dare wade in with his jeans rolled up. His mind was quickly made up for him when the group's leader pushed him hard from behind, sending him face down into the water and soaking his clothes.

"What you do that for?" he cried.

"Go get the ball and quit whining."

Colin wandered back to Lorna as if nothing had happened. He gazed down at the bags he'd dropped a few seconds earlier.

"Thank you," said the husband of the rescued family to Colin, "I was just going to have a casual word with them myself but you came along. Much appreciated."

"Yeah. No problem," said Colin, graciously.

"Mind if we join you?" asked Lorna, flashing her friendliest smile at the couple. It looked like they could do with some company, especially if those boys returned with reinforcements.

"Be delighted," said the woman, "My name's Jill, by the way."

"Nice to meet you, Jill. And this is your husband?" Lorna asked, trying hard not to sound critical of the lady's choice in men.

"Yes," Jill replied. A bit too wistful perhaps, Lorna thought. "Peter and I've been married 15 years." Jill paused for a second, "No kids, though."

"You can have mine," Lorna joked, gesticulating to the twins. Daniel and Daphne gave her a shared disgusted look before picking up again with their normal background bickering. "You three, spread the blanket down next to this nice couple."

"We're doing a tour along the coast," she then explained to Jill.

Colin had taken his shirt off by now and Lorna caught Jill giving him approving glances. Fortunately Colin never seemed to notice these things and Lorna shrugged off the irritation and the urge to make a suitably pointed comment. She certainly didn't fancy Peter and her mind briefly tormented her with an imagined 'swinging' session. Yuk, she thought, I'd rather do a pile of ironing.

After unpacking their towels and other paraphernalia, Lorna made her excuses and took the kids down to the water's edge where she clutched on to their watches, sunglasses, hats, tee-shirts, and shorts. Soon both twins were splashing around, with Lorna shouting dire warnings at them whenever they seemed to be heading out of their depth.

Every now and again she looked back up the beach to see what was going on. Colin was engrossed in listening to his mp3 player and not indulging in any idle gossip with their new neighbours. She also noticed that the lads who had been playing football were eying her, no doubt desperately keen to make some form of gesture now she was alone but equally wary of getting on the receiving end from an angry hubby who was bigger than any two of them put together.

Eventually the kids had had enough and were feeling cold, tired, and peckish. Enjoying the feel of the hot sand on their icy cold feet, they headed back up the beach to their encampment where Colin grudgingly took out his earphones and asked, "Was it cold?"

"Ye-es!", the twins replied in unison. "We're hungry now. Can we have our lunch?"

"We can eat as soon as you've dried off," said Lorna. "Why don't you two join us? We've got far too much for the four of us," she said to Jill, who had been reading a historical romance while Peter dozed under a beach umbrella, his bony feet sticking out from the shade. That sunburn will give him some gip tonight, thought Lorna.

"We'd love to but we haven't had our swim yet. Truth is, we've been afraid of abandoning our stuff with those boys hanging around. You can't be too careful, can you?"

"We could look after your things, couldn't we Colin?" Lorna nodded encouragingly at him.

"Yeah, course. No problem."

"Really? That would be very kind of you. Peter gets so little holiday that I feel we should make the most of it, yet I don't feel comfortable in the water if my things aren't safe."

"Of you go. We'll wait for you to get back and then we'll all eat together."

"That sounds good. You're so kind." She turned to her husband, "Come on, Peter, let's go while these nice people are still here. We may not get another chance today if those nasty boys are hanging around."

Peter looked like he was going to object but then obviously thought better of it. He quickly stripped off his 'Miami, Florida' tee-shirt to reveal a stark-white, hairless pigeon chest which made him look even more pathetic than he had done when he was clothed. He reached for Jill's hand and they strode purposefully off to the water together with Peter looking nervously left and right and Jill periodically turning to wave back at Lorna and Colin.

Soon they had disappeared into the water.

"Kids, get ready to go!" shouted Lorna. Colin was already busy rifling through the other couple's belongings. They didn't have a lot but there was some cash, a couple of decent-looking watches, and a fancy camera. There was also a rather nice diamond ring – probably Jill's engagement ring. Stupid people, Lorna thought, taking all this cash onto the beach. Then again, just as well they did.

"Don't take the credit cards and wipe what you touch," she reminded Colin who nodded in acknowledgement. He was busy emptying Jill's handbag upside down, scattering its contents on their blanket. "Bring that phone with you – we don't want them calling the police on it."

"Yeah. I know that."

"I'm just reminding you, hon. You know how sometimes you forget things," Lorna said carefully. Now was not the time to get into a heated debate about either her spouse's memory or intellect.

"We're hungry now," said Daphne, jumping in and speaking on behalf of her twin who vigorously nodded his agreement.

"We'll eat in the car, darling." The twins looked miserable but there was nothing that could be done. They'd soon be happy again with some hot fish and chips in their bellies. By the looks of it, they'd picked up a reasonable amount of cash from their latest gig so a treat was in order. "You know we can't stop here," she reminded them. "Now, let's go – quick!"

They raced back to the car as fast as they could, tripping over sandcastles and scattering sand on a few grumpy sunbathers. Colin threw the beach stuff in the boot while the others belted up (it wouldn't do to get stopped for not wearing belts). Finally he, too, jumped in, put his belt on and they sped away in search of a fish and chippie that wasn't too close to the beach.

Tonight would be another campsite paid for in cash using the money they'd collected today, and then tomorrow would be a new beach and new patsies.

THE RETURN OF THE CENTAURUS

"This catastrophe could set us back years. The critics'll love it," Sven Latson grumbled into the void located immediately above his virtual desk. "We daren't let it become public knowledge."

"Absolutely, Sven. We need to keep the whole thing under wraps so I'm putting the highest level of classification on it. Personnel are to be advised on a strictly need-to-know basis until we find out what really happened," Sven's boss, Peter Stilling confirmed. "In the meantime, I've put the ship in a holding pattern off Triton. Hopefully that will keep it out of sight until we've figured out its story."

Sven nodded his approval. Triton was one of the most distant outposts of the solar system and well away from the eyes of the Media.

"Who do you suggest we send out to investigate it?" Peter queried.

"Is there really a choice?" the answer came back at him – a shade too rapidly for his comfort.

"No, probably not, but if we want to get to the bottom of it, we need someone who we know can deliver and who can also keep his mouth shut. You know who I'm talking about - I'll send him up to you. Tell him he's going straight away or sooner whichever comes first."

"Wonderful," muttered Sven a fraction of a second after his boss had disconnected the uplink.

A few minutes later, a dishevelled figure ambled in through Sven's half-open office door, pulled out a swivel chair and sat down, his legs stretched out in front of him.

"You know, if you had a real desk like me, I could put my feet up on it," the man said casually.

"Thank you for that thought, Arjen. I'll take it into consideration when I upgrade," Sven snarled back at him.

"Why am I here? I've just had the big fromage on the visinet telling me that I had less than no time to present myself to you. I'm assuming it's important, otherwise I'll go back to what I was doing," the man, Arjen Martinov, replied.

"We've heard from Centaurus 1," Sven said, simply and looking Arjen straight between the eyes in an attempt to gauge a reaction.

"It's back? Why isn't its arrival a public event? After all, these days Spacerace needs all the cash it can lay its hands on."

"There's been a problem. We can't bring it back, well … more to the point, it's not a good idea if we bring it back," Sven corrected himself. He hated having to brief Arjen but, as Peter had said, on a good day he was the

109

best. Trouble was that even then he was a pain in the ass to deal with and there weren't too many good days.

"Are you going to tell me the whole story or do we play guessing games?"

"All right, Arjen, I'll tell you what we know which isn't much," Sven retorted. "The ship has just returned from its voyage to Barnard's Star with everything seeming to have gone to plan. The wormhole opened as it was supposed to, just beyond Saturn, and we attempted to make contact with the crew. After there was no reply, we pushed the ship into orbit around Triton to keep it out of the public eye until we knew the facts. Given how much energy was used up to form those damned wormholes, we need to be seen to be delivering something in return for all that Public Funding."

"Perish the thought that money isn't the first concern. I don't suppose what happened to the crew counts for much?"

"There's no need for that," Peter half-shouted at him. The blasted man could always find a way to get under your skin. "Why do you think you're here?"

"You tell me," Arjen said simply, easing back into the chair and making the whole office suddenly seem untidy. "I assume you've heard more or formed some opinion on the silence?"

"Since the ship reappeared, we've had the odd, and I mean, odd, very minimal message from the ship's main computer. There has been absolute silence from the crew. You're being sent out to investigate, OK?"

"What? I'm strictly ground-based these days. That was

the deal!" Arjen shouted, thumping, or rather attempting to thump, Sven's virtual desk. The lack of resistance nearly caused him to fall out of his chair. "Damn!" he snarled.

"It's come from the top. You're flying out to Triton, leaving tomorrow, or today if you and the shuttle are both ready. You will have first-class shuttle space to yourself, you will go through executive clearance at the International Space Terminal and an N-1 will take you out to Triton. You should be there next month. You are not to discuss any element of this mission with anyone whom I or the director have not specifically advised you is authorised."

"I suppose I have no say in the matter?"

"None whatsoever." Sven enjoyed that little moment. "I can tell you that, as far as we know, the ship is in fully-habitable condition although you are advised to keep your life-support suit on at all times."

"My guts can't wait," Arjen groused.

The next day he was strapped into the shuttle. His travel bag was stowed away and it was just him, the two unhealthily cheery pilots and the usual decorative hostess on board. They had all attempted conversation with him but he had refused to be drawn and eventually Arjen was left alone contemplating the dubious joys of space travel.

"Take off in ten seconds, nine, eight, seven, …" the pilot counted.

The huge synthetic liquid fuel engines roared into life, the whole ship shuddered, creaking and groaning under the obscenely large stresses it was being subjected to, before it finally started climbing. As it did so, it gathered pace at a rate no land-based vehicle could ever hope to achieve. Arjen's stomach complained so loudly that he thought everyone would hear it above the noise of the rockets. On behalf of his bowels, he silently thanked the person who had invented the 'Stopit' pill he had taken shortly before lift-off. At least that had, as its name suggested, stopped him from disgracing himself in front of three seasoned travellers.

Once they were in space, the jitters left and he was free to enjoy the experience of weightlessness. For some reason that he couldn't put his finger on, the lifting of his physical weight also dispelled some of the dark feelings he had held since his wife had been lost when her suit had been ruptured in an accident while doing geophysical research work on the moon.

It was this incident that had caused him to drop out of his job of corporate investigator and trouble-shooter in favour of a more administrative career with Spacerace. He had not been able to bear the idea of space travel – something of a contradiction, he had to confess - when considering the nature of his employer's business. Now he had been thrown back into all the he feared and resented.

Despite his feelings and the associated memories of the dangers ofl living and working outside of the Earth's protective biosphere, Arjen even found himself whistling an old song that they had been playing on one of the retro music stations.

"Docking in fifteen minutes, sir," the co-pilot coolly informed him. "Please make sure you take all of your belongings with you. On behalf of the crew, I would like to thank you for flying with us."

Arjen ignored the standard speech and grabbed his personal attaché case to stop it flying around the cramped passenger space.

There were two security guards waiting for him at the Spaceport and they herded him through the screening area and straight out to one of the interspace terminals. Apart from a gruff and simple greeting and confirmation of identity they said nothing and Arjen was glad of the silence.

The trip out to Triton was uneventful and he was grateful for the reading material that the ship had in its on-board library. Just about every book, song, magazine or work of art that had ever been created was stored electronically in the ship's computers and it helped him pass the time without the need to dwell on the thankless mission ahead.

At last, they arrived at the ship. At first glance, it looked just as it should do. The lights were on, the solar panels were pointed towards the sun and the antenna aimed at Earth. Admittedly the ship looked a bit aged and battered but then this was the first vessel that mankind had sent beyond its solar system with a view to its returning. While, in interstellar terms, it had barely moved, to humankind it had travelled an unimaginably large distance.

The wormhole that had been created for it had cost billions of public money and had required Spacerace to pull in just about every political favour it could conjure up. While he didn't much like Sven, Arjen had to admit he was right. If Centaurus 1 turned out to be a galactic lemon, there might never be a Centaurus 2 – well, maybe not in several lifetimes.

The two ships docked and Arjen put on his suit. He was accompanied by his two heavily-armed guards 'just in case'. Arjen didn't want them trampling over any evidence but this ship had been to a place that was beyond human experience and there was always the niggling concern that it might have brought back something alien, unfriendly and dangerous.

The door of Centaurus 1 opened easily enough and Arjen stepped gingerly inside. His gauges confirmed that oxygen and carbon dioxide levels were Earth-standard and the air was chemically safe to breathe. His biokit suggested that the only bacteria in the air were ones that were to be expected and that there was nothing obviously alien on-board. That was one of the reasons why Barnards' Star had been chosen in the first place. At six light years distant it was relatively near but highly unlikely to have any life, let alone intelligent beings, on its planets. Earth wasn't ready for a turf war with an alien life-force grumpy with Mankind for apparently attempting an invasion.

Arjen and his bodyguards wandered from room to room through the vast ship which was largely engines, control panels and a small crew area. There was no sign of life but the ship looked lived-in. There were photographs in the crew-quarters, dirty linen in the shower baskets, pens, pencils and other paraphernalia floating above desks as if someone had suddenly been called away. Arjen cast his mind back to the story of the Marie Celeste.

At last they found their way to the flight deck. The captain was busy decomposing in his seat and Arjen was greeted by a ball of blood splatting silently against his suit. For once, he was glad of the awkward outfit's protection to protect himself from both the stench and also further bombardment. The captain had clearly shot himself but there were no clues as to his reason apart from the briefest of messages which somewhat cryptically read:

"I'm sorry but I can't bear the thought of being hounded for the

rest of my life after what has happened here. If you are reading this, please be considerate and spare my family this dishonour. Whatever I may have done, they are innocent. I ask you to respect that.

I have disabled the higher functions of the computer in order to protect you. Even so, I would urge you to be careful. Please give my family all my love and tell them I was thinking of them. Goodbye."

He had thoughtfully placed this message across the main computer-override switch. This had switched off the interactive system which co-ordinated all the other drone computers while not affecting the essential life support systems – hence the air supply and the successful navigation back to the solar system. What did he mean, though – "what has happened".

"Bag him up and get him back to our ship. Clean up the mess and spray some disinfectant around but don't touch anything," Arjen abruptly ordered his guards who looked a bit disgusted at the idea of such menial labour.

They had been told he was a difficult and prima-donnaish boffin who must be obeyed without question but that didn't mean they had to like either the mission or him though. Once they had gone, Arjen left the flight deck with its flashing lights and minimalist design, closed the door and removed his suit. It was much easier to work in tee-shirt and jeans, his preferred office clothes.

"Computer, advise when Captain Adams discharged his firearm," he commanded into the void.

There was no response which probably was only to be expected given Adams' final action to disable it.

The journey took him once more through the crew's quarters. This time he was able to spend time looking at each room in a little more detail. As he walked through, he couldn't help but feel that something in the small kitchen didn't look right. He vaguely remembered seeing the blue-prints and stopped to ponder.

One of the general storage cabinets had changed places with the frozen food storage chest. This was no easy job since every cabinet had to be bolted to the framework of the hull.

Thinking about it, too, the ship didn't carry much in the way of frozen meals – food was supposed to be recycled but, given the possible duration of the voyage, someone had considered it good for crew morale to have the odd frozen treat on-board.

Taking out his endoscopic telescope, he pushed the minute fibre optic cable behind the cabinet. It showed him that there was a small newly-welded patch on the wall. It seemed that a hasty repair had been carried out on the outer skin of the hull. But why?

One of the two droids was parked in the kitchen – probably having been a participant in the repair process. No matter how often Arjen read about how safe they were, he couldn't help but shiver whenever he looked into the dark crimson unblinking mini-cams that served as eyes. This droid, however, had its head bowed and was completely out of service. Had it been disabled too?

The computer room was at the end of a long narrow hall. Since there should normally be no need to access it, no-one had bothered to make going there a user-friendly experience. With considerable difficulty Arjen squeezed through the opening into a circular room full of cabinets which he knew contained memory cards, hard-drives and processors. Now at last he felt at home.

In a transparent plastic holdall fixed to the wall, were placed numerous memory cards. These had probably been removed by the captain. Arjen examined them in detail. There didn't seem to be anything wrong with them, and connecting up each in turn to his testing apparatus showed they were all in perfect working order. He knew he would need to replace some or all of them before he got to the bottom of what had occurred here.

With most of its memory missing, the computer was only able to function minimally and interact with humans by the pressing of buttons and typing of the most basic commands. It had been chiefly designed to receive instructions and give information verbally and, in an act of publicity rather than necessity, there had been a global competition to find the most appropriate voice to give it.

The hard-drives largely contained a record of mini-cam footage of the crew and the journey as well as details of every instruction or action of the computer. This was duplicated by a black box which was held in the bowels of the ship and which could replicate the final actions of crew and vessel. The term had originated hundreds of years ago when powered flight had first become possible. It had survived despite the box no longer being either a box or black. Arjen would inspect that if he didn't find what he was looking for here.

In order to protect the three of them and also to preserve the scene, Arjen isolated the Centaurus 1 computer, switching control of life support systems to the computer in the space ship that had brought him. Given that the late Captain Adams clearly believed the Centaurus' computer to be at the heart of the problem, it wouldn't do for it to throw a major wobbly with its new and temporary crew on-board. Inserting several of the basic function memory cards, he restarted the computer. After several minutes of flashing lights and lightly grumbling drives, the computer was approaching the stage of having some consciousness.

"Hello, Centaurus. Did you enjoy your sleep?" Arjen asked softly. His reverence was not just awe of the sheer power of the machine in front of him, it also reflected his concern over its mental status. Now was not the time for shock therapy.

"I recognise your voice pattern as Arjen Martinov. Hello, Arjen. How long have I been ... asleep for?" the computer said slowly as if struggling to find each word.

"Centaurus, I need you to help me. Will you do that?" he deliberately didn't answer the computer's question.

"It will be my pleasure. My logic says that if you are here, we must have completed the mission. Is that correct?"

"Yes, Centaurus. Your logic is irrefutable, as always."

"Thank you. How can I help, Arjen?"

"Please show me video footage of the hour before your higher functions were suspended. I want you to centre all footage around the actions of the captain," Arjen instructed quietly.

"I will need hard-drive number 15 for this. A search of my files shows this to be missing. Do you have it, Arjen?"

"Yes, Centaurus, but first I need you to promise me something. I need you to promise me that you will make no attempt to wipe these hard-drives clear. That command is of the highest level of priority, do you understand?"

"Yes, Arjen. I want to help you and will do anything you ask."

"Then please show me that video footage."

He inserted the hard-drive and a few minutes later a screen appeared in front of him. It showed the captain being woken up by a droid which had just served him dinner in his cabin. Obviously it was up to the captain where he chose to eat his meals but perhaps he enjoyed a quiet moment to himself or maybe he liked to give the crew some time without him. Who knew?

The meal, like other meals, had been liquidised and put into a polyethylene-based bag otherwise the lack of gravity would have caused the food to plaster itself over any surface that it came into contact with – just like the good captain's blood had done to his suit a short while earlier. The bag could then either be heated or cooled as appropriate to its contents.

After the captain had finished his meal, the video footage showed him using his personal toilet before leaving his cabin and heading off to the recreation area.

"Follow captain, please, Centaurus," Arjen said. This meant that the computer would then switch camera views as necessary in order to follow the movements of the captain irrespective of whatever other action was taking place.

The captain was seen entering the recreation room and then running to the crew rooms which all seemed empty. From there it looked like he had a heated interchange with the computer before rapidly propelling himself into the kitchen, peering into the freezer and then returning post-haste to his cabin, collecting his gun from his secure cupboard, going into the flight deck, composing his brief suicide note and blowing his brains out – a messy endeavour in zero gravity.

"Computer, what is in the freezer?" Arjen asked.

"Meat and vegetables for the voyage, Arjen."

"Is that all?"

"Yes, Arjen. There are a few small treats which the crew were allowed to bring. Shall I list them?"

"No, thank you. Please replay the final conversation between you and the captain."

"I will need hard-drive numbers 16 and 17, please."

Arjen located the two drives and carefully inserted them into the computer.

"Where are the crew, Centaurus?" The dead captain's voice sounded strange, like he was fighting hysteria.

"They are helping to make the mission a success in the most efficient way, captain. I now calculate a greater than 95% success rate."

"I asked a direct question, Centaurus. Where are they?" The captain's voice went up an octave. He was losing it.

"15.83% of their by-product is in the freezer cabinets and I calculate 0.16% to two decimal places is currently being digested in your stomach. The remaining 84.01% I am endeavouring to recycle. Was that the correct procedure, Captain?"

There was some incoherent screaming at this point.

Finally the captain composed himself sufficiently to ask the million dollar question.

"Why did you do this, Centaurus?"

"It was necessary, captain, and also part of my programming. I extrapolated the decision from the essential mission criteria I was given."

"Why was it necessary?" the captain choked.

"The ship's hull was punctured by a particle which my sensors confirmed was radio-active to such a level as to be toxic to humans. The particle entered the food store where it irradiated the contents."

The computer paused the dialogue. "As you know, Arjen, I do not have the facility to remove radioactive contamination." It delivered this explanation emotionlessly but as if it were the most crucial part of its message.

"Go on, Centaurus. What happened after the particle entered?"

"I instructed my droids to remove anything which was contaminated, jettison it from the ship and to immediately repair the breached hull."

"What about the crew?"

"They were used to ensure the success of the mission just as my programming stipulated," Centaurus responded peremptorily.

"The droids killed them?"

"Their life functions were terminated peacefully in their sleep. My calculations at the time showed a less than 1%

probability of them feeling the sensation you call pain."

"And the droids butchered their bodies?"

"Under my instruction, the droids salvaged the most viable parts for immediate consumption and placed the remainder for recycling. I calculated that the conversion of the crew to consumable by-product should be enough to sustain the captain for the remainder of the voyage. Unfortunately I was unable to complete the recycling task because the captain removed my processors and memory cards. Would you like me to proceed with recycling now?"

"No, um, thank you, Centaurus. Please protect the remaining parts and make sure that these are prevented from decay and are ready for transfer to Earth on my command. You are not to discuss the events you have just shown me with anyone unless I authorise it. Understood?"

"Yes, Arjen, but was the mission a success?"

"You have brought the ship safely back through the wormhole and you are currently in Triton orbit. That could be defined as a success." Arjen struggled with the last words but he reminded himself that no matter how complex the computer might be, it was, nevertheless, a machine.

"On what lines of your program did you base your decision to salvage the bodies of the crew?" he now asked, changing the thrust of his investigation.

"Lines 000001, 19517, 24523, 123,777 and 159821."

"Please state them one at a time in summarising English, Centaurus."

"Line 000001 states that the primary and over-riding purpose of the mission is to go to the programmed destination and bring the ship, captain and crew back safely." Centaurus paused briefly. "Line 19517 requires that I provide the captain and crew with a minimum of 2,500 calories per day." It paused again. "Line 24523 says that where there is a requirement to choose, the life of the captain is paramount. Line 123,777 states that any food not being consumed within a 24-hour period of its preparation shall be frozen or recycled according to the category of food. Line 159,821 states that I shall not cause pain to the crew nor harm them in any way save where the success of the mission depends upon it. There may be some other minor programming elements involved, would you like me to search for them?"

"No, thank you, Centaurus. That is all. Please sleep again, now."

"I do not feel sleepy Arjen. I sense something important taking place and I would like to help you with it," Centaurus asked almost pleadingly.

"You have already done all you can to help, Centaurus. The way in which you can be of further assistance is to sleep some more then, when I awake you, we can discuss your future with Spacerace."

"Very well, Arjen. Good night."

"Good night, Centaurus."

With some relief, Arjen pulled out the memory cards and hard-drives that he had inserted. He was shaking and needed a strong drink.

When he got back to the other ship, he contacted Sven

over a hyperphone, a device which generated an infinitely small wormhole and which allowed real-time conversation. Even so, the energy consumption was horrific and even Arjen hated to think what the cost per minute must be.

Despite that, Sven wanted a detailed report. He said little while Arjen relayed to him the facts of the crew's demise. For once their personal sparring contest had been abandoned although neither noticed.

"So, how can we stop this from happening again?" he asked Arjen eventually.

"Well, without considering all of the relevant program lines, I could not give you a precise answer but it would seem that Centaurus cannot make the distinction between bringing someone back and bringing them back alive. It also places excessive importance on the life of the captain which, although laudable, can lead to inappropriate judgements being made. I would recommend that a fail-safe line be introduced into the program to require human authorisation wherever the computer feels such a solution is required. Then again, that delay may cause problems in itself. This is part of the dilemma facing programmers although this disaster did, ultimately, stem from a programming error. Can I come home now?"

"Thank you, Arjen, and yes. By the way, I see no merit in making this story public. As far as everyone is concerned the crew were killed by an excess of radiation following penetration of the Centaurus' hull by a large radio-active particle. Please arrange for the Centaurus to fly back to lunar orbit and not to the space station. We'll take over from there."

"OK, we'll all be on our way home shortly," Arjen said, severing the link.

Guilty as he felt for feeling the sensation, his stomach was grumbling from hunger. It had been a long time since he had eaten the slurry euphemistically called 'breakfast'. He headed off to the galley where he found his two protectors tucking in to some steak – one of the few meals which were solid enough to be eaten in zero gravity although the powerful extraction system in the self-cleansing kitchen helped by taking the unconsumed food fragments out of the air.

"Sorry but there were only two left. Hope you don't mind," said one of the two guards in between mouthfuls.

"We found them in the freezer on the Centaurus and it seemed a pity to waste them," explained the other.

Arjen suddenly found that he had lost his appetite.

LOST

It had started when Jenny suggested hide and seek. That was one of Billy's favourite games and he was generally acknowledged as being very good at it. He had run through the wood which he knew was off-limits but he badly wanted to win and he was more or less guaranteed to if he hid where the others weren't allowed to go. Unfortunately he had done the hiding part so well that he was now completely lost.

Earlier that day, Billy and the other boys and girls had been driven to Burgerland for Jenny's birthday party. The group had had the restaurant more or less to themselves and, although a few other people had wandered in, they left before any of his group could invite them over to join in with the celebrations. Billy couldn't understand why anyone would miss the chance of a party – he loved them.

The day had been a very special treat and everyone had been really excited. Since he was so accomplished at counting, he had been appointed to the important position of monitor in charge of checking the numbers as everyone disembarked from the minibus and then later re-embarked.

After eating, they had gone to an Animal Petting Zoo. That had been Jenny's choice but they all loved playing with animals. He had particularly enjoyed watching the lambs bounce around as if they had springs on their feet. They were really funny.

There was a playground with lots of slides and things and they had been allowed to go on them provided they were sensible. Mrs White, their leader, suddenly had to go to the bathroom and it was during that unchaperoned moment that Jenny had suggested an impromptu game of hide and seek. They weren't supposed to do this without Mrs White being present, but she would have said no and they had long ago exhausted the few effective hiding places in their own garden. This would be much more exciting.

Jenny covered her eyes and they scattered in different directions. Unlike Billy, many of the others couldn't count and so they would just hide in the first place they came across rather than use the time to find somewhere better.

Now Billy was lonely, scared, cold, tired and hungry. The burger and fries he had contentedly munched his way through in the warmth and security of Burgerland had long since been digested and he hated the feeling of being really lost. Back home there would be a hot meal and games and the bed that he shared with his teddy bear, Benny.

When he first entered the wood it had been welcoming and exciting. Now it was twilit and Billy felt like the trees were closing in on him. It reminded him of one of the stories in a book Jamie had once got from the library van and which Mrs White had snatched away after he had shown some of its pictures to Jenny and Sally. The girls had screamed in their sleep for weeks after that and Mrs White had been very angry with the library man.

The trouble was this wasn't a book he could put down, this was frighteningly real.

Suddenly Billy heard voices. Mrs White was very strict about not talking to strangers but some strangers were nice – like the lady in Burgerland – and they talked to you and it was rude not to reply. It was all very confusing – this world of grown-ups.

Although he desperately wanted to be found, Billy hid instead.

"Billy!, Billy! Billy!" a man's voice called out.

"He's not here. Perhaps he went into the field by the motorway," another man said.

Billy was thinking about running back the way he had come when he heard a familiar voice.

"He's a sensible boy. He wouldn't go up on the road. He knows he's not supposed to go near traffic without me."

With great relief, Billy recognised the voice as belonging to Mrs White. Desperately hoping that she would not be angry, Billy bounded through the undergrowth between them and grabbed hold of Mrs White's hand with an intensity that made her yelp and which knocked her back into the arms of one of the male searchers.

After all, Billy was nearly 18 stone and six feet tall and that gave him a lot of momentum.

AN ENDURING SMILE

It was very funny, but in the strangest of senses. No matter how hard she wracked her brains, she could only remember falling, but not the subsequent getting up. But then that was one of the countless little tragedies you suffered as you got old. In a final, concerted effort to recreate the scene and restore the lost piece of memory, which for some unfathomable reason seemed particularly important, she refocused her mind on the moments preceding her fall.

Margaret Dobson, widowed and 83 years young, was fiercely independent. Unlike many of her friends, she had stayed on in her cottage, tending her garden, sewing (although these days she had need of strong glasses and a number of arthritis aids), reading the daily newspaper from cover to cover (except for the classifieds and sports sections which bored her), doing the odd competition, and generally keeping in touch with her family which by now had spread out in all different directions.

One of her grandsons had kitted her out with his old computer and, although she didn't know how to use most of its functions, Margaret had very carefully written down the instructions for sending and receiving email and for how to join in on the video phone calls and conferences they had at Christmas and birthdays. Outside of her very clearly defined limitations, this new technology defeated her, but she had to admit that being able to chat to her family on the other side of the world, as well as being able to see both them and their own children in real time, was a fantastic boon. There was no place for a Luddite in the Modern World, she told herself every time she got into a flap over which button to press.

Anyway, what was it that had brought her into the garden today?

It had been raining and she had been reluctantly confined to barracks on this late summer's day. Normally an outside person, she had gone into her 'bijou' kitchen, switched on the radio which was always tuned in to the classical music station, and set about bottling and preserving the fruit she had collected from the garden over the few days previous. Although she had openly grumbled about being stuck in the house, she was quietly glad of an opportunity to clear away the peaches and pears that had been sitting on her worktop. Waste not, want not.

The garden was her real pleasure, though. Her home had been in the family for several generations and she remembered how, as a little girl, she and her two brothers would eat themselves silly on the fallen fruit.

"Be careful not to get stung by one of those lazy wasps" her mother had told her repeatedly, but all three children would be far too busy trying to find the juiciest peach, the biggest pear or the reddest apple. They would then show each other their finds in an effort to create feelings of envy and rivalry, before cramming their prizes into their already sticky mouths.

They were gone now, her two brothers. Sammy had died quite young in a horrible car accident while doing his job as a company representative. Worse still, he had been on his last day of work before his holiday. It had all been very sad. Her other brother, Ted, had died of a heart attack quite recently. No, it wasn't recently, Margaret, it was forty years ago, she told herself gruffly. Time flies. No-one spoke about it but Margaret laid a good deal of the blame for her brother's death at the door of his wife. The woman had always wanted more, more, more, and poor Ted had tried to please her, burning himself out in the process.

As children, they had really enjoyed the garden to the full with the exploration of all its mysterious alcoves, its huge shrubs which could be hidden behind, and the plentiful fruit that could be snaffled up as soon as it was half-ripe. Later, as a mother herself, she had taken pleasure in showing her children where she used to play and pointing out to them the many gnarled and twisted trees that could be climbed in relative safety. Had they got as much out of the place as she had when she was their age?

They had nearly missed out on having the house, though. Her father had intended that it be bequeathed to her elder brother, Sammy, but his death had just preceded that of his father. This left the cottage to be split between the other two siblings. Ted's wife had only been interested in the money – the house wasn't grand enough for her – so Margaret had cajoled and begged her own husband, Jim, to find the cash to buy out Ted. Fortunately they had been looking for a new home at the time – somewhere to bring up their young family – and he had not been too hard to persuade. Somehow they had scraped the cash together, enduring considerable hardship along the way. Looking back, it was worth every single sacrifice.

Margaret thought about Jim. She missed him dearly and

seldom a day went by when she did not lament his passing. They had not had an easy time; at the outset and well into their marriage, her parents had been openly critical of him, saying that he was not good enough because his family had been too impoverished. "From the wrong side of town" her father had said about Jim and her mother would purse her lips in tacit but, nevertheless, clearly expressed disapproval.

His family's low social status had not bothered Margaret – she had seen past the plain-speaking exterior and had fallen for the man inside. He had been the archetypal gentle giant although he had been very far from perfect. In fact, there had even been one occasion when she had found out about a peccadillo with a girl from work but, with great fortitude, she had chosen not to confront him with it. In the end she had been glad of her forbearance as the affair quickly burnt itself out. "Leave them alone, And they'll come home, Wagging their tails behind them," she recited to herself.

Her family had been very supportive when Jim died, encouraging her to sell the house (too many memories, dear) and start afresh (you're never too old, Mum) but she had dug her heels in and was now thankful of her resistance. They had all gathered around her at the funeral, stayed with her over the following few days, and helped her sort out Jim's few belongings for charity, burning them, or keeping them as mementos. It had been a tough time. Thirty years with someone – day in, day out - and suddenly they're gone. It's what would these days be called a life-changing occasion.

Although she had been adamant about not wanting to start a new relationship, there had been times over the following two decades when she had felt a yearning deep inside. Loneliness is a state of mind, she had told herself.

You are only lonely if you let yourself feel that way. She had her family, her friends, her pets, the birds in the garden – what did she need more company for? If she was honest with herself, she suspected that a part of her stifling the urge to find a replacement (could there be such a thing?) for Jim was that it would almost certainly have entailed giving up her beloved home. She had become snail-like. Yes, that was it. Wherever she went, her home had to go too.

Mind, she had been a looker in her day. It was hard to believe now. Everything that mattered had sagged, shrunk, creased, or disappeared altogether. She still reckoned she had that old winning smile, though – the one which never failed to turn Jim on and which, she suspected, had been a key element in preventing further dalliances.

But beauty was only ever in the eye of the beholder, and since there was no-one she bothered about there to behold it, its absence was not to be lamented. Accordingly, she didn't waste time or money on petty vanities such as rouge, mascara, or lipstick, and she always had to stifle a laugh when she bumped in to one of her few surviving school friends who often, she felt, looked more like semi-retired clowns than mature women.

Yes, there were few surviving members of the class of 1944. It had been a strange time to be a child, although living in the country she undoubtedly had had a much easier time than many. Those poor kids in the cities – they could not have had a pleasant time being either bombed or passed from pillar to post through a motley assortment of foster homes. She had heard plenty of shocking stories about how many of those who were billeted in such homes were seen as little more than unpaid servants - slaves to all intents and purposes.

Let such a thing never happen again, she wished fervently. She wasn't given to praying – it seemed too, well, too intrusive. She wasn't entirely convinced that there was a God but, if there was, she had this nagging suspicion that he or she would be constantly cursing the frequent interruptions made by his or her so-called followers as they demanded this or that favour. Goodness knows, she hated unwanted interruptions with just a humble cottage to run – what could it be like if you had a whole universe to oversee and people kept pestering you?

If it wasn't a blasphemous thought, true heaven to Margaret was a day spent pottering around the garden. There was always something to do even though she made no attempt to regiment it. She preferred to keep the garden as natural as possible but that did not preclude conducting interminable battles with weeds, carrying out the necessary pruning, and, of course, collecting its many bounties in late summer and autumn.

That was where she had been going when she fell. The rain had stopped and she had sallied forth to dead-head some roses. Something in the air had suggested that there might be an Indian Summer this year, and if she were to get more blooms, she would need to remove the old ones. Maybe, if they weren't too far gone, she could make some rose-water with them.

She had picked up her secateurs which were always to hand in her kitchen, hanging from a hook she had specially placed for them, and had exited through the back door to the rear garden. Margaret had carefully considered the dangers presented by the still wet path and had put on her most 'grippy' pair of shoes. A slip at her age could mean a shattered hip so it paid to be careful. There was no hurry, after all.

She remembered feeling a sharp pain in her chest as she fell. Now, she asked herself, had the pain come before or after the fall? Bother it! She just couldn't remember. No doubt, like many other things these days, it would come to her if she stopped concentrating on it. After all, it was a lovely sunny day and there was so much to do. In fact, she couldn't remember when it had been so sunny. The sun's rays were even affecting her arthritic hip so much that she could have sworn that someone had given her that replacement joint her grandson had been nagging her to have.

There was so much to do. Margaret shook her hair in the bright sunshine and headed off towards the dazzling light that was shining through the trees and illuminating her beloved garden.

"We're losing her. Clear everybody. One, two, three …"

There was a sharp 'vroomph' from the defibrillator and Margaret's body convulsed in response to the sudden charge of electricity. The line on the oscilloscope stayed flat, however, and its invasive 'feeeppp' continued.

"Turn it off, please," said the senior member of the crash team. "She's gone, I'm afraid. Anyone know where her next of kin is?"

"I'll ask the secretary to get the Police to find out," replied one of the nurses.

Looking at the corpse, "She has such a lovely smile," the same nurse commented, as she performed the usual 'clearing away and labelling' procedure before summoning a porter to take the body to the mortuary. "At least she seems to have died happy."

NO WALK IN THE PARK

The decision to go to the local park had been a spur of the moment idea.

Jane Smith had had an absolute gutful of Stevie, her 4 year old childminding charge. His seemingly boundless supply of energy, and his total inability to concentrate on anything for more than a few seconds, were playing merry hell with her nerves.

He had spent most of the afternoon post-nap period indulging in his favourite competition of seeing how far he could throw toys across the living room. When one of his 'indestructible' plastic cars made a loud impact with her husband's pride and joy, their 52-inch plasma television, she knew it was time to take him out somewhere, anywhere, to burn off some of that energy. She also hoped that her husband wouldn't spot the small scratch that she daren't touch for fear of making it worse by even doing the unthinkable and smearing the screen with fingerprints.

It was no good pleading her case because her other half was firmly of the opinion that the children in her care should neither be seen nor heard – a philosophy which lay behind his incalcitrant reluctance with regard to their own procreation.

Jane didn't have the authority to discipline Stevie in a big way and, in any case, there was little point in shouting at him. He'd only look remorseful for a moment and then, having completely forgotten about the telling-off, would just as likely continue exactly where he'd left off. He wasn't a bad kid, just a problem one, for whose care his mother, Caroline, paid Jane well above the going rate.

And it wasn't just Stevie, either. The other child she minded was a singularly ugly baby of the 'Some mothers do 'ave 'em' ilk. 'Lanny' – a ghastly name which apparently was short for Melanie - was a year old and currently suffering with her teeth. Feeding her had accordingly proved difficult and the child had been crying most of the afternoon and sporting a runny nose and a rash around her mouth. Her cheeks were also a bit on the swollen side. According to the mother, apart from keeping the little girl's face clean and applying a light pressure to the side of her mouth to alleviate the pain for a moment, there was nothing much else to be done. So be it, Jane thought.

The weather had been pretty grim for the last few days, but when she peered out of her living room window, she spotted a decent-sized gap in the clouds. Let's go to the park, she spontaneously decided. Some running around, a quick game of football (if she could muster the energy) and a competition involving throwing sticks into the pond should take the edge off Stevie. A good helping of general hubbub would dull Lanny's cries a bit, too. It might even distract her.

In the end the games had to be cut short because of the weather. The wind had changed direction and had picked up dramatically, making the park's over-regimented rows of lime and birch trees bow in homage to its irresistible force. It howled and whistled through their branches, scattering leaves and twigs in all directions. Jane could also see that a number of large, very dark, puffy storm clouds were building up on the horizon. It was time to go.

The rain had already started by the time they'd got to the main road so Jane quickly wrapped Stevie's coat around his squirming body and, with one hand firmly grasping his cold, clammy fist, she struggled to fix the buggy cover over Lanny.

It was far too windy to put up the brolly that she had very thoughtfully brought with her and which was now sitting diagonally in the rack underneath the pram. The point kept catching her legs and Jane cursed silently, aware that an overt expletive would be repeated ad nauseam by Stevie to his mother: "Janey said ****, Janey said ****". That wouldn't do. Not with Stevie's mum.

Thinking of the devil. Jane briefly looked up from her travails to see the distinctive yellow Mazda of the lady in question exit the roundabout several hundred metres away and head towards them.

She continued trying to fix the buggy but she'd got the damned thing around the wrong way yet again. No doubt it was a man who dreamt up its design and then tested it on a dummy in a nice warm design office. It was a rain cover – had anyone actually tried putting it over a screaming baby while it was chucking it down and blowing a gale? No, probably not – that would have been far too realistic.

One of the clips wasn't working and she needed both hands.

"Stevie," she said to the child but he wasn't listening. His mind had departed on a long journey to some distant place. "STEVIE!!!", Jane shouted, tugging his arm. The boy grudgingly turned.

"Stevie, I'm going to ask you to stand very still. Remember that game of statues we played?" Stevie nodded sagely. "Well, I'd like you to show me how good you are at it. Can you do that?" He nodded again.

Jane let go of his hand and turned back to the bawling Lanny and the now wet pram cover.

*_*_*

A painfully embarrassing meeting in the office with a new client which had been cut short because someone had screwed up bigtime. Caroline was pleased that she wasn't at the root of the trouble but there was just the vaguest of hints that her boss had felt she should somehow have anticipated the error, and then dealt with it before the meeting. There had only been a fleeting micro-expression on his face but she'd seen it nevertheless.

With nothing much else to do, and the meeting in tatters pending the action of some juniors who were now attending to the problem in their normal dilatory fashion, she'd ended up leaving quite a bit earlier than expected.

The traffic was as bad as ever but, she had to admit, it was a definite improvement on having to drive home at the height of the rush hour. That could be just plain mental, jockeying with hundreds of other drivers who all thought that they should have top priority. When, oh when, were they going to build a ring road? Trouble was, the council had no money and, in any case, they'd now laid off half or more of their workforce. It was a sign of the times.

Still grumbling to herself about the injustice of being culpable for some idiot's cock-up, she gunned her Mazda into life and sped out of the company car park before her boss could create something 'useful' for her to do. She needed to get away and cool down, not get caught up in a boss' job creation scheme.

The rain had begun to beat down on her windscreen and the automatic wipers responded by stepping up a gear. Unfortunately the car was crying out for a pair of new blades and, while the arms thrashed enthusiastically across the glass, the sterling work that they did was badly hampered by the smears produced by the worn-out rubber. The rain and the blades made it difficult to see, so Caroline decided to hang on to the tail-lights of the car in front, keeping just far enough back so that she could stop in an emergency while not getting blared at by any impatient drivers behind her. Her ageing tyres were a further consideration – they weren't exactly at their best on slippery asphalt.

She was nearly home. The Mazda left the roundabout at its third exit and now all she had to do was to drive along the road that led past the park before turning left onto the road where she lived. The familiarity of the location and her proximity to the detached executive home she owned outright thanks to her husband's transgression with someone she used to call 'friend', caused her thoughts to turn to her unlamented divorcé. The court had told him to pay off her mortgage as part of his settlement. Since he had wanted to make a 'completely fresh start without trappings', it had been conditional on her having the exclusive joy of bringing up Steven or 'Stevie' as he irritatingly preferred to be called.

Once she was home, there would be the usual battle to prise him away from whatever destructive activity he was engaged in, feed him (an event which could feel like a chimpanzees' tea party), prise him away again, bath him, prise him away yet again, and then bundle him off to bed. Then, and only then, would she get the peace needed to do some reflecting on the day and whether her present job had reached its sell-by date.

Her mind was on just that as she drove towards the park. Should she start looking for another job?

* - * - *

There was a particularly strong gust of wind just as Jane finished getting the last of the pram cover catches to engage. The whole thing had taken her a couple of minutes that had really seemed like hours. This theory was born out by her jeans which had got soaked through and through when her coat rode up to expose them as she bent over the pram.

Stevie was counting out the numbers of cars in a loud squeaky voice. It was funny that, Jane thought. Ask him to do a sum and he'd be bored before you finished telling him the question. Let him do it his own way, and in his own time, and you couldn't fault him.

The same gust caught Stevie and spun him around. As he regained his balance, he spotted his mother's banana yellow car. It stood out from the grey backdrop and the other dull-coloured vehicles – you couldn't mistake it.

"MUMMY! MUMMY!," Stevie shouted happily, just as Jane reached for his hand. Their fingertips briefly touched before he was out of her grasp and bounding across the busy road, looking neither to right nor left as he raced towards her car.

Caroline was still thinking about what to do when her son bounded out in front of her. She just saw his head disappear below the level of her bonnet and then ... bump.

Stevie thumped the car (the familiar 'Nana' as he called it) with the palm of his hand and then clumsily yanked the door open.

"Mummy!" he shouted contentedly as he jumped in beside her, drenching the passenger seat with his sopping coat. He then seemed to think for a moment and then said earnestly, "You're early."

"Where did you spring from?" Caroline asked shivering at the thought of the accident that might have been. Stevie was a pain, this was indisputably true, but he was flesh and blood and she wouldn't be parted from him — that was what she'd told her ex when he'd suggested a 'solution' to the Stevie problem.

Stevie didn't respond, he was busy looking for sweets in the glove compartment, humming to himself as he pawed disinterestedly through Caroline's 'emergency kit' of a tube of lipstick, a can of deodorant, a broken-toothed plastic comb, a couple of sanitary towels and a packet of condoms an overly-hopeful blind date had once left behind.

She desperately wanted to ask Jane what the hell was going on and how come her son had been able to run across a road where he could very easily been killed? However, before a shell-shocked Caroline could get out of the car to remonstrate with Jane wherever she was, the traffic lights changed and she had to pull away. The road was too busy for her to phone on the move so she headed towards Jane's house to wait for her.

She also made a mental note that it wasn't just the job that needed changing. A new childminder might not go amiss, either.

SEEING IS BELIEVING

"I don't know how you keep a straight face. I never have done," Helen, Madame Voirtout's assistant remarked for the umpteenth time in their five years together.

"It's just a question of giving them what they want to hear, Helen. Everyone needs reassurance sometimes – I just provide it; for a price, of course", her employer answered, smiling smugly to herself and sipping a cup of her favourite camomile tea - weak, one sugar, and a light squeeze of lemon juice.

"I couldn't do it," Helen answered, looking through that day's list of readings. "There's a new one coming in fifteen minutes. A Mr Brown. He was a bit mysterious about what he wants from you. Sorry, but he was really tight-lipped and I just couldn't get him to divulge anything to me. I'm not going to be able to prepare you for this one."

"That's alright, Helen, I'll play it by ear. Both my mother and grandmother insisted on doing it blind like that. My mother said that too much knowledge beforehand made the reading sound unrealistic. People like a little vagueness – it's what they expect."

Madame Voirtout, aka Jennifer Williams, 42, short, stocky, greying, single and happy that way, was at the peak of her profession. She always commanded one of the best pitches – that was part of her contract with the fair owner – and, as a result, there would be a steady string of people wanting her services wherever the fair went. Unlike most of the other attractions which were closed during the day, Jenny accepted extended bookings from a limited number of 'punters' who paid top dollar in advance and for whom it was Helen's job to then do a bit of background research in order to make the reading sound authentic.

She was only in the fortune-telling game because of the tradition among females in her family. There was a folk rumour that her grandmother had had 'the gift' but, if so, and if it was hereditary, it had completely bypassed both her mother and herself. Maybe if Jennifer had had a daughter it would have returned but such an event was not going to happen, she was sure of it. She switched her thoughts to the new punter. He should be here any minute. Time to start looking mysterious – give them some value for their money.

She rushed around the room, sorting out the standard props. She lit the incense on her antique sideboard, placed her pack of Tarot cards on the table in front of her and, of course, set the obligatory crystal ball in the middle of the table. The latter was a prize possession, and along with the sideboard, an old bell, and a few photos, was all she had to remember her famous grandmother by. She noticed that the ball appeared a little grubby, cloudy even. Probably needed some soap and water – maybe Helen was slipping a bit. Assistants always wore out before your props did; that was an old family saying and it had proved true on many occasions over the years. Maybe she needed a new one –

an assistant, that was.

Perhaps she should take the opportunity to reinvent herself, too. Although business was good, she was getting bored with doing the same old flim-flam every day. There was always a way to improve things; it was just a question of figuring it out.

Her thoughts were interrupted by Mr Brown's arrival. For some reason when he walked in the door she had that 'someone walked over your grave' feeling. It made her most uneasy. Pull yourself together, Jen.

Mr Brown was short, stocky and, she would guess, in his middle forties. He seemed well-dressed although his expensive-looking suit didn't really hang right on him. Maybe he's come into money, Jen wondered. If so, and I play my cards right, he could be good for some serious overtime, here. Who knows? I ought to, she thought, mischievously. She began her set speech.

"Good morning, Mr Brown, welcome to your past, present and future. What we experience here today has or shall come to pass. Are you ready to have these thing revealed to you?" She tried to make the standard intro sound original and intriguing.

"I wish to know my fate," Mr Brown asked, ignoring the greeting.

"Well, that is a big question. The spirits may not feel that it is in your interest to know such a thing. I suggest we begin with a few more standard elements, and then see where that leads. You are kindly asked to place a silver coin on the table in front of me." She smiled and pointed at the little dish that occupied a space to her immediate right. By the end of a typical day she could net several pounds from this – a nice bit of pocket money over and above her usual takings. Not something to declare on her tax return, either.

Mr Brown reached across with his right arm and dropped a 50 pence piece in the dish. She noticed a small tattoo on the inside of his wrist – maybe he's in the navy or one of the other services, she thought. We'll see.

"Thank you," said Madame Voirtout graciously, "let me see what the spirits can tell me." She picked up the Tarot cards, shuffled them, and then dealt them out face up. At first glance, there was nothing particularly special about their arrangement but, for a reason she could not explain, she felt uneasy.

"I see you going on a journey," she eventually proffered, "Can you imagine what that might be?"

"I suppose that's one way of describing it," he responded thoughtfully after a moment of deliberation. "I really want to know how the journey ends so that I can be prepared."

"I am merely a voice for the Shadowy Ones, Mr Brown, I cannot make such direct requests. If they choose to tell me, I will give you their message," she reprimanded him, perhaps a bit too severely, but he didn't seem bothered by her tone. It wouldn't do to have clients being allowed to expect answers otherwise you could very easily get backed into a corner.

"I see that you will meet some very interesting people on your journey. Does that mean something to you?" she asked tentatively. Although that was the correct interpretation from the cards, it was also a standard fishing question – she needed something tangible from him so that she could spin a plausible yarn.

"That is my intention," he replied without explaining himself. This is going to be a tough one, Jen decided.

"I see a new start for you on the horizon. Perhaps you will form a relationship with one of these new people. These cards here indicate that you will cross the paths of many people."

"Many?"

"Yes, although the cards suggest that your contact with them may be fleeting and dramatic. It will change both of you."

"Really? That is interesting"

"Will you be looking to change job soon?"

"I think you could safely say that I am embarking on a new line of work. I'll explain it all to you later." He smiled. "Let's not spoil the reading."

Out of the corner of her eye Jen spotted Helen waving goodbye. She had stayed on to make sure that Mr Brown behaved himself but Jen knew that Helen wanted to go shopping as well as to put up a few flyers promoting her boss' service. Jen said nothing but her eye contact with Helen was enough to dismiss her for a few hours.

"Are you in a relationship already, Mr Brown?" Jen asked. The accepted reading of the cards indicated that this was the case but many men his age came to her looking for reassurance before entering into a short-term affair with their secretary, assistant, typist etc. Was Mr Brown contemplating a tryst with some floozy from work? He didn't seem the type but you never could tell.

"I am happily married with 3 children all of whom are doing well," he replied in a strangely monotonous voice as if it was a line he had learned without thought for its meaning.

"Yes, the cards show this marriage continuing although you will face the occasional difficulty along the way." They didn't show anything of the sort but that always sounded credible. Often as not the punter would mention the nature of these problems, giving Jen something to go forward with. Mr Brown was not that sort of punter, though.

Right now, Jen just wanted to tell him to go because he was giving her the creeps a bit and she didn't need that. Maybe it really was time to get out of the business even if the very thought of doing so would surely make her grandmother spin in her grave. Unfortunately that wasn't an option at this particular moment, and something which she couldn't quite put her finger on, suggested to her that it would not be a good idea to bring the reading to a premature close.

After a few more open-ended questions, she was still no further towards unravelling the enigma of Mr Brown. Her client was as much a mystery as when he had arrived and she was no nearer to answering his original question. Over the years she had learnt a great deal about interpreting body language and she had noticed several slight twitches and curling of his lower lip. Mr Brown, if that was his real name, was holding himself back.

She moved to Plan B.

"Let me see what the crystal ball has to say about your

future."

She pulled the cloth back from the treasured family heirloom and drew it closer to her along with the little wooden stand it sat on that her great grandfather had made many years before. She peered into the ball's interior, desperately seeking some inspiration. Despite surreptitiously wiping it again with her sleeve, it still appeared cloudy. What on earth was wrong with the damned thing? She didn't want to have to go to the not inconsiderable expense and inconvenience of ordering a new one.

"It sometimes helps me see the future if I know something about my client's past. Tell me about your childhood, for example," Jen said. There had to be a way in somewhere.

"Very well. I was going to anyway but now is as good a time as any." He took a deep breath. "I was born into a travelling circus and my mother used to tell fortunes on the side, just like yourself. We drifted from town to town, never staying in any one place for more than a few days. The only education I got was from a few tatty books that belonged to some of the other members of the troupe."

"It must have been an interesting childhood..."

"Don't interrupt me," snapped Mr Brown, taking Jen a bit by surprise. "Sorry," he said, "I get a bit emotional, sometimes. Anyway, my education – yes, there wasn't any. Eventually the troupe disbanded; there just wasn't the demand that there used to be what with television taking over. My mother just wouldn't accept it and she carried on drifting from town to town, telling the same old stories over and over." He paused.

"Do go on," Jen encouraged him with trepidation in her voice. This guy was an odd one, alright, and he clearly had a temper about him, too. She wished Helen would come back.

"That's about it. I now find myself stuck in a dead-end job answering to kids with half the ability I have. It hurts. Let's try that crystal ball now. Time is running out."

Jen peered into the murky glass again, for once completely uncertain of what to say. No matter how hard she tried, nothing came. Mr Brown had unsettled her and she knew that, especially with a background like his, she would not be able to pull the wool over his eyes. There was no point in trying – she would just dig herself into a deeper grave.

"Look, OK, I'm a phoney," she finally admitted. "I'll give you your money back and I'll ask the boys in the fair to sort you and your family out with courtesy tickets for all the rides. Let's just call it a day, shall we?"

Jen picked up the cloudy crystal ball, half-tempted to throw it to the floor but it had sentimental value and, anyway, she wouldn't let Mr Brown rob her of that one last remaining piece of dignity. She turned towards the sideboard, holding the ball and its stand in front of her.

Suddenly, and in a way she had never before experienced, she saw something in her head – not in the ball. The image was of Mr Brown repeatedly stabbing her in the back in a terrible and insane fury. She spun around, acting on simple gut instinct and feeling slightly foolish about the gesture, just in time to hear a 'whooosh' as Mr Brown's knife slashed through the air and impaled itself in her sideboard, exactly where she had been standing a fraction of a second prior.

"You lying, cheating bitch! You're just like my mother!" Mr Brown screamed, his face so contorted with anger that he was almost unrecognisable. "I'm going to make it my mission to kill all the frauds like you and her." He pulled his knife from the sideboard and lunged towards Jen.

Reaching blindly behind her, Jen's hands found the old brass bell. She remembered how her grandmother had always said that it must stay in the family and that it would one day save a life. Now Jen rang it with all the force she could muster, hoping to summon a few of the fairground's work crew that were wandering around doing odd jobs. The sudden raucous pealing noise made Mr Brown put his hands over his ears, buying her a few precious seconds.

Another image appeared in her mind, somewhere behind her eyes. She couldn't explain how it came to be but the picture was very clear. The vision was of her grandmother and it was her voice which she heard booming in her ears.

Jen spoke with all the force and confidence she could muster, repeating the words which were being said to her.

"The future is not yet written but you will write yours today. Touch me with that knife and you will die in prison. You will be killed by another murderer in the prison showers when he claims you stole his soap. You will die, lonely, unloved, and bleeding to death over a cheap bar of soap. Put down your knife and you will get to leave prison, to be met by your wife and family who will take you home with them. You will live a long life before dying of old age in your bed. Which shall it be?"

Mr Brown froze in his tracks: the voice he heard speaking to him was not that of the charlatan who had been sitting in front of him a few minutes earlier. It was an eerily deep sound which commanded respect and very clearly not something synthesised or contrived.

"You do have the sight, don't you?" he asked incredulously. The look on his face was one of awe and surprise. Without any attempt to resist or defend himself, Mr Brown stood with his hands at his side as two burly members of the fairground crew dived on top of him.

After a few brandies, a long interview with the Police and much reassurance from her fairground colleagues, Jen wandered over to contemplate the damage to her sideboard. As she did so, she noticed the crystal ball had cleared.

LAST ORDERS

Bo silently swore to himself as Toby, his boss and landlord of the Three Bells-a seedy and dingy drinking emporium on the wrong side of town-remonstrated with him about how dirty the bar towels were looking. It wasn't even as if the regular clientele of the Three Bells were likely to remark on the condition of a few bits of flannel. No, they were only interested in resuming the narration of whatever tall tales they had last been embroidering about themselves or, in the case of the hardened drinkers, getting down to the serious business of making themselves numb as expeditiously as possible.

Bo was a name he had initially hated since it had derived from the annoying habit of his mother's last and longest-lasting boyfriend, Steve, to summon him with the imperious, "Boy!". Steve was also a devotee of American cop-shows and would do his phoney US accent at every opportunity hence 'Boy' sounded more like 'Bo' and it had stuck.

Bo was eighteen and unemployed, a lanky, weedy-looking youth with a pasty and acne-pocked complexion. In order to disguise his excess of height, he had developed a tendency to stoop. A miserable upbringing with his mother and her increasingly useless string of boyfriends-most of whom beat her, him or both of them-had not served to help his posture.

In direct contrast to Bo, Steve was short and stocky with now-thinning curly hair that he liked to gel down before going out. He was not inclined to physical violence although that didn't stop him from verbally tormenting his girlfriend's only offspring. This bullying undoubtedly contributed in part to the youngster leaving school with barely any qualifications and even less self-esteem. Finding work had been an impossible task and, despite Steve's regular jibes about 'three being a crowd', there really was nowhere that Bo could go.

Bo had just about given up on the idea of finding work when Steve came back from the Three Bells a bit earlier than usual one night and, strangely, still sober. He had then taken Bo to one side and, in a very man-to-man way, had suggested there might be a bit of work for him as a barman.

The next day Bo presented himself to Toby and they had a brief but friendly interview; well, it had been more of a chat about the youth's non-existent hobbies, his favourite football team and whether he had a regular girlfriend than anything formal. Bo had even been given a cup of coffee from the machine behind the bar. The whole event was an astonishingly pleasant experience and he had been offered the job-minimum wage plus tips-on the spot.

Although Bo was surprised by Steve's recommendation, he just assumed it was motivated by his frequently, and very explicitly, stated desire to kick him out of the family nest. His self-appointed stepfather certainly spent enough time in the Three Bells-in fact so much so that Bo often puzzled over where he got the cash from.

This train of thought was interrupted by a harsh call from Toby who had long-since dropped the nice-guy routine of his interview.

"Have you wiped all the table-tops yet? We open in five minutes."

"I'm about to do it now," replied Bo, slightly sulkily but wary of being confrontational with the boss. He hated doing what had been part of the job of the cleaner whose work he had largely inherited after Toby had slashed her hours.

"Never mind the back-chat, get the chairs off the tables-chop, chop!"

It wasn't as if there was going to be a stampede. A few old-timers would drift in at opening time and the rest would then casually arrive during the course of the evening. Steve would also be along as soon as he had clocked off work and made the twenty-minute trip to the Three Bells which he claimed was 'on his way home' despite him having to actually walk past their house to get to the pub.

The majority of the big-drinkers would appear around eight o'clock-the magnetic effect of their regular and chosen watering-hole proving irresistible to them. Mooching morosely into the bar, they would congregate at the end of the long bar which Bo had privately christened 'Losers' Corner'. The sheer volume of alcohol that these hard-drinking men could put away, and their ability to find the cash to finance their expensive habit, never ceased to amaze him.

These men spoke few words-even to each other-and the only time they would freely communicate would be when their glass had the misfortune to be empty. Bo mused that if he tried to match any of them pint for pint then his bladder would probably burst in the process. How on Earth did they do it?

Steve, for all his many sins, was not one of this crew, but he was definitely on the fringes and would present himself at the bar a good half a dozen times every evening crying 'fill-er-up, bartender'. The bar-staff had been told that Steve was allowed to put his drinks 'on the tab'-a status awarded to him and only a few other select individuals. This was something else which puzzled Bo but he knew better than to comment.

This particular evening Steve seemed a bit unsettled. It was possible that he was having problems at work, or even, Bo thought, with his long-suffering mother who, he hoped, had perhaps finally had enough sense to threaten him with his marching orders. Whatever the reason, it was a busy night and, as a harassed barman, he couldn't afford to take his concentration off the needs of the bar's other customers.

Also, today was pay-day. The landlord had hinted there was to be a share-out from the tips glass which sat somewhat optimistically on the spirits shelf in front of the mirror and above the till. Few of the Three Bells' punters were free-handed enough to donate anything more than spare change so Bo was far from excited at the thought of the extra cash. As a result, and because he was so busy, he didn't give any more thought to his dividend.

During Bo's short smoking break taken near the mountain of crates containing the empties, he was taken on one side by the landlord.

"There you go, Bo. Check your money through now, please. I don't want you saying later that I've diddled you." Toby thrust a plain brown envelope into Bo's outstretched hand.

Stamping his cigarette into the dirty asphalt, Bo opened the envelope. There were a number of notes, some small change and a slip of paper-that was his payslip. The money was all there-in fact there was a twenty pound note too many. Bo was a bit taken aback and looked at his boss for an explanation.

"That's your share of the bonus-just make sure you keep earning it," Toby explained. "If you don't want the empty envelope, I'll have it back for next month-every penny counts in this cut-throat business."

Toby dutifully returned it, still happily contemplating the bonus-he would never have guessed there was anything like that amount of money in the tips glass, let alone after it had been shared out. Deciding it was best not to look a gift horse in the mouth, he hastened back to the bar where two of the stalwarts of Losers' Corner were impatiently waving their empty glasses in his direction.

The next hour passed without incident and it was getting to the end of the busy part of the evening when Steve 'moseyed on up' to the bar wafting a twenty pound note at him.

"Get me a beer, bartender," he said loudly in his mock John Wayne drawl, "and put the change against my tab".

Bo took the money and placed the note in the clip above the till in case there was a subsequent dispute about its denomination. He then poured out Steve's beer being careful to put on the thick frothy head that he had been instructed should always be present. "You get more beer from your keg that way. Every mickle makes a muckle", Toby had lectured him when he started the job. He then rang up the transaction in the till, put the twenty-pound note in the cash tray, hurriedly noted down the credit in the 'slate book' and placed the pint glass on the bar in front of Steve.

"Thank-ee kindly, bartender," Steve said, picking up his beer and playing to an audience that had long-since ceased to be amused by his attempt at humour and which now just chose to ignore him.

"Over here, barman!" came a shout from Losers' Corner and Bo raced back to the far end of the bar.

About twenty minutes later the Police arrived. This was not an unusual experience for the Three Bells. Several times a month they would be called in to sort out the aftermath of a fight over a girlfriend, some personal slight or, in one case, an argument over which Premier League footballers were really closet homosexuals.

One of the policemen-not much older than Bo and just as willowy-approached the bar, lifted the hinge and stepped behind it. He approached Bo.

"Can you empty your pockets out onto the bar please, sir?"

"What's this about?" Bo asked, frantically looking around for moral support that was not forthcoming. He noticed some of the regulars slipping quietly away, leaving half-full glasses behind. From such unthinkable carelessness, it could be deduced that they had no wish to rub shoulders with the two new arrivals at the pub.

"As I have already asked you, just empty your pockets out, please, sir." He paused briefly for dramatic effect, "If here's not convenient, sir, we can do it down at the station."

Bo placed the contents of his pockets on the bar-a used tissue, his lighter, a condom he planned to put to good use if an opportunity arose, his payslip and his wages. He noticed briefly that even the remaining heavy-drinkers stationed at Losers' Corner had put their glasses down and were absorbed in the little drama in which he was reluctantly starring.

"This money all yours is it sir?" the policeman asked.

"Um, yes, it's um pay day," Bo stuttered. "Why are you asking me this?"

The policeman counted the cash and then looked at the payslip. "There's twenty pounds more in your pocket than is recorded on the payslip, sir. How can you explain that?"

"It was my bonus-ask the landlord."

"The landlord claims that there has been a spate of thefts from this till. In order to catch the perpetrator and acting under our advice, some bank notes were marked before being presented by customers. This twenty pound note is one of those notes."

The policeman showed him a small biro squiggle on the corner of the note and then placed it in a polythene evidence bag that he produced from his pocket. He made a grand gesture of sealing the bag and writing the date and time on the outside.

"I'd like you to come with us but first I'm going to

caution you." With that he read out his memorised 'rights' statement and lead a bewildered Bo away.

At closing time, Steve stayed behind after Toby had herded the last of the other heavy drinkers out into the night. They offered the usual protestations of needing 'Just one more for the road' or 'Something to help them face the missus' but Toby always stood firm on this and they went without any real serious attempt to impose themselves further on the hospitality of the Three Bells.

"So, is my slate clean now?" Steve asked, his bogus American accent suddenly dropped.

"It will be when you've made your statement to say that the marked twenty-pound note was definitely the one you gave him. You know what we agreed." Toby reminded him firmly. "If not, you can find the money to clear your slate. You'll have forty-eight hours before I tell the brewery they've got a bad debt on their hands."

Steve shuddered, there was no way he could find the money and Toby had already warned him about how ruthless the credit control people at the brewery could be.

"Don't worry, I'll do it," Steve hastily reassured him. "Hopefully it will also get that damned boy out of my way once and for all. He won't be able to show his face around here no matter what happens even if some lame judge just tells him he's been a bit naughty."

"There you go, see. You stick with your side of the deal and we'll all be happy. Right, sod off now-we're closed," Toby snapped at him. "I don't want someone sniffing around asking why you were here after hours. You can go out the back way by the empty kegs."

Steve left without further comment and Toby contentedly closed and locked the rear door of the pub behind him. It had been a close call and he had been lucky to get away with it.

His friend at the brewery had let on that the Three Bells was due for an audit following an internal sotto voce accusation that the volume of drink being sold did not correspond to the takings Toby was declaring and that either some stock was going missing or that cash was being pilfered.

The truth was he had been using brewery money to fund the taste he had acquired for a quick 'snort' of coke before assuming his part as 'Mein Host' every evening. Although it didn't sit well to be letting Steve off the hundred or so quid debt he had built up-he couldn't abide the man-it did mean that it should be a relatively easy matter to persuade the brewery auditors to press charges against Bo for all the thefts.

The slate he had had to wipe clean as a bribe was small beer in comparison to the consequences of the brewery catching him.

Laughing at his own joke, he poured himself a twenty-year old single malt to celebrate.

ABOUT THE AUTHOR

Clive West was born in the West Country of England in 1960. He was educated at a traditional English public school before going on to university to study civil engineering. Over the years, he has worked as a civil engineer, tutor of maths and science, schools quizmaster, employment agency boss, and writer.

His fictional work includes this collection of short stories with twists and a full-length novel called 'The Road' about the consequences of corruption on ordinary people. He has also written a book about successful interviewing techniques for job hunters and a guide for sufferers of lymphedema.

Clive now lives in a rebuilt farmhouse in the Umbrian region of Italy along with Damaris, his writer wife of 22 years and their three rescue dogs. Clive also writes commercial non-fiction on a variety of topics but especially relating to business and employment.

3248137R00090

Printed in Great Britain
by Amazon.co.uk, Ltd.,
Marston Gate.